Legacy of Magic

LEGACY

BOOK ONE

DENISE CARBO

For my dad. He is missed every day.

Prologue

Tendrils of mist snaked along the forest floor. The full moon guided her hurried steps. Foreboding drenched her senses. Nerves taut, Josephine paused beneath a towering oak and placed her palm against the ridged bark of its massive trunk—seeking the comfort it usually bestowed. Fear and urgency shrouded her like the dark cloak she wore. Her gaze searched the murky path behind her.

Nothing stirred.

An eerie silence stretched across the dark woods. The scurrying and calls of night creatures were absent. Josephine took several small steps forward. She was already late.

Her coven waited. They needed to decide on a plan of protection and detection. Two members had already mysteriously disappeared. Fear ran rampant throughout the coven. Some whispered they were under attack. By whom, they didn't know. But why, they could guess.

Power. Their coven comprised twelve of the most powerful witches ever born—each a master in their discipline of the four elements.

Delicate ferns flicked at her ankles. A branch snatched the edge of her hood and halted her progress. Josephine freed the material, only to have another branch snag in her hair. She stood motionless and examined the path ahead. The clearing where they always met wasn't too far away. She could be there in just a few moments. She studied the plants along her path. Branches, twigs, even the leaves were arching onto the trail, blocking her way.

Dread snaked across her senses and intuition. Something was wrong.

She took a cautious step back. Her hand covered the precious life already growing inside her. A rare vision had shown her the child she carried. She wasn't even a month along.

Ominous shadows thickened. The hairs on the back of her neck rose. Evil had been done in the forest this night.

Josephine clenched her fists over her womb. She would not risk this cherished gift. She veered back toward her home. A twig snapped behind her.

She didn't look back. She ran.

A spell whispered from her lips, "Plants of the Earth, hear my call. Protect our flight. Hide us from sight." She repeated the words three times as she continued to run.

Roots broke through the ground behind her to hinder the steps of those who pursued her.

Branches and vines stretched across the path to hide and block.

A plan formed in her head. She and Adam would disappear. Her husband had mentioned relocating from England to the American colonies before, but she'd always been resistant. She hadn't wanted to leave her coven and all that she knew. Their baby must come first. She'd move to the ends of the earth if necessary.

She would have to bind her power. There was no other way. Those seeking her would sense it and find her. She must lock away her magic until it was safe to pass on to her child.

Chapter One

"Time to face facts Cory, you're lost." Cory glanced down at the car's navigation system for the dozenth time in the last half hour. She didn't recognize any of the street names. The GPS had directed her off the highway and onto back roads, each smaller than the last. Nothing looked familiar.

"Take the next left," the English sounding navigation voice intoned.

"Left? What left? I see trees," she mumbled.

Granted, it had been quite a while since she'd been here. Not since she was a kid. The last few times she'd seen her, Aunt Addy had traveled to her parents' home in New York. If she remembered correctly, her aunt's house was perched on a small hill on a corner. There were a few other houses on the road. The town should be just a short distance away. So where on earth was she?

There...was that a road? Good grief, is that dirt?

Sure enough, the next left was a dirt road. Cory made the turn and stopped. Should she turn around? Maybe she should go back and find some civilization and ask for directions. The map looked like it opened up to more streets ahead. Should she chance it?

Why not? Live a little.

Cory crept down the road. There were no potholes or ruts. It was in pretty good shape. At least she wouldn't damage her car. The last thing she needed was a car repair bill to put a drain on her savings. She was on a tight budget until she could get a job.

Ooh...a mailbox, and another just ahead. So maybe she wouldn't end up as a headline after all. "Woman lost in the wilds of Connecticut." She snickered. Who knew Connecticut had wilds to get lost in?

Cory glimpsed pavement ahead. "Yahoo," she muttered.

Two turns later, she loosened her tight grip on the steering wheel and relaxed against the headrest. She might be headed in the right direction after all, and if not, there were at least houses around if she got into trouble.

"In a quarter of a mile, take a right-hand turn." The disembodied voice was really getting on her nerves. Whoever decided a snooty, nasal, English voice was the way to go, anyway? It was like having an old professor lecturing her on the proper way to drive. Personally, she'd like to hear someone soothing yet confident, like a Southern drawl or an Irish lilt.

Cory looked at the map on the navigation screen to read the name of the road. Clarkhill, that's Aunt Addy's road. Finally.

The squeal of tires jerked her gaze back to the road. A neon green sports car barreled straight for her.

She yanked the wheel to the right and slammed her foot onto the brake pedal. Her BMW hit the dirt on the side of the road and slid out of her control. Her white knuckles gripped the steering wheel as the small car rocked back and forth gently before stopping completely in the shallow ditch running parallel to the road.

Someone wrenched her door open. "Are you hurt?" The gravelly voice echoed from somewhere above the roof of her car. She stared at a pair of jean-clad thighs before whispering, "I don't think so."

"Then do you mind telling me what the hell you were doing driving on my side of the road," the harsh voice demanded?

She gasped and pried her fingers off the steering wheel. Her fingers ached slightly. "Your side? What were you doing driving like a bat out of hell?"

A pair of furious, ice-blue eyes suddenly appeared in her line of vision. "What speed I was driving wouldn't have mattered a damn if you had been on your side of the road!"

Cory clenched her hands in her lap and glared at the man. One arm rested on her roof as he leaned down to give her a withering glare. Rich black hair fell haphazardly around his head in a complete absence of style. Five o'clock shadow darkened his strong jaw, despite it being nowhere near five o'clock. In the back of her mind she registered she would find him quite handsome if she wasn't so pissed off at him.

"Back. Up," she uttered through clenched teeth, as she disengaged her seatbelt and began the arduous and ungraceful process of climbing out of her car. Luckily, he complied and shifted to stand at the side of her tilted vehicle. He offered her his hand, which she ignored. As she finally made it out and stood beside him, the realization dawned she needed to look up quite a bit to meet his gaze. One dark brow shot up while he scanned her from head to toe.

She spotted his car parked on the shoulder of the opposite side of the road. The sports car didn't look to be suffering any damage. What was he complaining about? She was the one sitting in a ditch, and she refused to believe it was her fault. "I hope you have insurance."

He folded his arms across his middle and leaned back against her car. "It's not my insurance you need to worry about, sweetheart. It's your own."

Sweetheart? Of course he blamed her. Probably for the simple fact she was a woman.

Insufferable man.

"Take a look at those skid marks between your car and mine." He gestured to the road with a lift of his chin. "Those wider, deeper skid marks are mine. Notice they're all on my side of the yellow line. Now take a look at yours, the narrower set. Which side of the line do they start on?"

Crap!

Damn it. Okay, she had looked down at the GPS, but only briefly. Cory closed her eyes and sighed before turning back to Mr. Tall, Dark, and Annoying. She really, really, hated to eat humble pie.

"I might have drifted slightly onto the other side of the road," she grudgingly admitted. "But if you hadn't been driving so fast, my car wouldn't be practically on its side in that...trench right now."

"Perhaps if you knew how to drive, your car wouldn't be in a ditch."

"Listen, you male chauvinistic—"

He held up a hand and interrupted her. "It has nothing to do with you being a woman, just a bad driver. Now, go stand out of the way while I check out the damage to your car."

"Why you arrogant—"

"Do you want to get out of this ditch or not, lady?"

Cory stalked to the front of her car. The smell of burnt rubber scented the air. She wiped her clammy palms on her jean clad thighs.

Her foot started tapping as he got down on the ground to look under her car. It rested at an angle, making it easier for him to examine the undercarriage. He just assumed she knew nothing about cars because she was a woman. How did he know she wasn't an expert? For that matter, what did he know? He could make matters worse, and then where would she be?

He stood up and wiped his hands together. "Doesn't look like you bent the axle, but you're going to need a tow truck to get you out of here. You should have it fully checked out before driving it again. There's a decent garage over in Bensonhurst, about an hour north of here."

"What about Allendale? That's where I'm headed."

"You're in Allendale."

She inwardly sighed in relief. "Oh good, isn't there a mechanic around here?"

The man smirked. "Yeah, but I don't think you'd want him working on your car."

"Why not? He's not any good?"

"Oh, he's good, but he's also picky about the cars he works on and doesn't take kindly to being called chauvinistic, arrogant, or run off the road test driving a six-figure car for a client."

Double crap!

Fine, Bensonhurst it is. Time to regroup. First, she needed to find a way to get to her aunt's.

Cory walked toward her car to get her cell phone and insurance information just in case there was damage to his car, or the client's car. "I'll give you my insurance information, so you can be on your way."

He stood next to her car with his hands on his hips while she scrambled to the glove compartment and back out, grimacing as she bumped her knees against the console, and handed him her insurance card.

"New Jersey? What are you doing in Allendale?"

"Visiting my great aunt." She pointed to her insurance card. "Can you just take a picture of that with your phone?"

He frowned down at her card. "Your aunt wouldn't happen to be Adelaide Stone, would she?"

Was the town that small? "Yes, why?"

A harsh sigh accompanied him handing back her insurance card. "Because she happens to be my neighbor, and she said her niece was coming to stay with her. Come on, I'll give you a ride."

He walked over to the green sports car while she stood there debating whether to accept the grudgingly offered ride or stay and try to call a tow truck or taxi, or something. Did they have taxis out here? It would probably be better to get to her aunt's and then figure out how to get a tow truck out for her car. Her rude rescuer was already opening the driver's side door before she made her decision. Cory grabbed her purse and hightailed it across the road—before he changed his mind. If she was completely honest with herself, she couldn't really blame him if he did. But who said she wanted to be honest with herself?

Trees and houses with large yards passed by in a blur. Silence hung heavy in the confined space of the sports car.

She should say something to relieve the tension. Not an apology. She'd rather suffer the silence than apologize to the condescending, arrogant jerk. If he hadn't been speeding, it wouldn't have been an issue if she had drifted over the line for a split second.

Before Cory could come up with something to say to diffuse the tense situation with her aunt's, and probably her, neighbor the man drove into the driveway of the old Victorian her aunt called home. It was a grand old lady, white, decorated with ornate trim work, and a large wraparound porch. The gardens she remembered surrounding the home were in disarray and overgrown. Her mother was right. It was getting to be too much for Aunt Addy to take care of. Well, she was here now, and she could help.

Cory extended her hand to her newfound nemesis and reluctant rescuer. "We've gotten off on the wrong foot. Since we're going to be neighbors, why don't we let bygones be bygones? My name is Coralea Bishop."

He stared at her outstretched hand, making no move to shake it. She was about to drop it and give him another tongue lashing on his rudeness when he smirked and enveloped her hand with his. His skin was warm and rough from calluses, and it swallowed her hand whole.

"Finn D'Orsey."

"Thank you for the ride, Mr. D'Orsey." He was already sliding out of the car, so Cory scrambled to do the same. Apparently, he planned to accompany her into her aunt's. Was he planning on tattling on her? For gosh's sake, she felt like a child about to get in trouble. Well, if he was going to tell on her, she was going to tell on him. So there. She wanted to stick her tongue out at him, and if he had been in front of her instead of in back of her, she would have.

The door opened as she approached the front steps. She looked up with a bright smile ready to greet her aunt, only to find a tall, handsome blond man in the doorway. He was dressed in a white button-down shirt with the sleeves rolled back and black trousers. He stared piercingly at her for a moment before a welcoming grin spread across his face. Wow, someone should bottle that allure. They'd make a fortune.

"You must be Coralea. Adelaide has been waiting, eagerly, for your arrival." He stepped out onto the porch and took hold of her arm, gently directing her into the house. "I'm Sebastian Marks, Adelaide's lawyer, and friend, I hope." He completely ignored Finn D'Orsey.

Sebastian led her through the two-story foyer into the living room to the right of the stairs. Little had changed over the years. A floral covered sofa and two wingback chairs were grouped together on an oriental rug in front of the marble fireplace. The smell of jasmine reached her, and she spotted the teacup on the table next to her aunt.

"Look who I found," Sebastian called out.

Aunt Addy craned her snow-white head in the entry's direction. A wide smile bloomed across her face. She placed the papers she'd been perusing on the small, round table next to her chair and grasped the arms of the chair to help her rise. "Oh Coralea, I'm so glad you made it. I was beginning to worry."

Cory hurried forward to greet her aunt with a kiss against her soft cheek. A hint of lilacs surrounded her. A pale, pink, button-down blouse and tan slacks adorned her slight figure. "I'm sorry to make you worry, Aunt Addy. My GPS decided to take me along the scenic route."

Twinkling blue eyes stared into her own. They were the same height and shared a strong family resemblance. Is this what she would look like in another fifty years? If so, she considered herself lucky indeed.

The older woman grasped Cory's cheeks with her cool palms. "Oh, just look at you, more beautiful than ever."

"I must concur," Sebastian murmured behind them. Her aunt spared him a small smile, which transformed into a wide, welcoming smile. "Finnegan, I didn't know you had arrived too."

Finnegan? Cory glanced over her shoulder to find he'd come up behind them.

"Hello, Addy." He stepped forward and kissed her opposite cheek, brushing up against Cory. "I actually arrived with your niece. Her car broke down and luckily, I happened by."

Broke down? So, he wasn't going to tattle and gloat after all? What was he up to? Did Sebastian's presence have something to do with his attitude? She glanced over at Sebastian to find him frowning at Finn and Aunt Addy. No. She doubted he would care about that, but Sebastian didn't seem to care for Finnegan. Why? Was there a reason, other than his abrasive personality? Perhaps she should keep a close eye on her new neighbor. Aunt Addy seemed awfully fond of him, though.

"Don't worry about it. The tow truck is already on its way to haul it to my shop." Finn patted her aunt's hand where she grasped his forearm.

"Wait, what?" She must have missed part of the conversation. Was he talking about her car? When did he call a tow truck, and what happened to sending her to another mechanic an hour away?

Finn stared at her with one eyebrow raised, just daring her to say something.

"Oh Coralea, you're so lucky Finnegan found you." Aunt Addy took Cory's hand. "Now, you must be tired from your ordeal and all the driving. Why don't you go upstairs and freshen up? I've prepared the guest room to the left for you. It's bigger than the one you used as a child, and it has its own bathroom entry. Once you've rested, we'll catch up."

"Thank you, that sounds wonderful." She was tired, and more than happy to escape from having to make an attempt at polite conversation with Finnegan and Sebastian. What was up with those two, anyway? They still hadn't said a word to each other or acknowledged one another's presence. She'd have plenty of time to figure it out later, if she was so inclined. As long as neither one of them was taking advantage of her aunt, she didn't really care if they hated one another.

"Mr. Marks, it was nice meeting you." Cory nodded in his direction.

He crossed the short distance and took her hand. "A delightful pleasure meeting you, Coralea. I hope we can get to know one another very soon." He smiled and kissed the top of her hand. His hand was smooth and cool to the touch, a distinct contrast to Finn's.

Was he flirting with her? It had been a while, and she was out of practice. A charming gentleman to be sure, and a handsome one to boot. Perhaps things were finally going her way.

She looked at Finn. "Mr. D'Orsey, thank you for your assistance. I assume I'll be hearing from you about my car?"

The corner of his mouth lifted in a smirk. "You assume correctly."

Condescending jerk! He should take some charm lessons from Sebastian. To think she was now obligated to him for the ride, towing her car, and hopefully fixing the thing. God help him if he messed up her car. If Aunt Addy wasn't here and didn't seem to like him so much, she'd tell him not to lay a finger on her car just for principle's sake.

Cory gave him a tight smile and started for the stairs. He was really helping her out, and she was trying to be gracious about it, but did he have to make it so damn hard? It was clear he was only helping her because of her aunt. Granted, she had run him off the road and given him a piece of her mind. She wished she'd given him a swift kick to his well-shaped ass. Not that she had noticed or anything. All right fine, she had noticed. She wasn't dead or blind.

CORY LAID down on the queen size bed in the guest room and stared at the ceiling. The royal blue quilted bedspread cushioned her. She absently rubbed the soft fabric between her fingers. Her aunt said to rest, but she didn't feel like sleeping. She'd only latched onto the excuse to escape her frustrating new neighbor, who made her want to hit him. She couldn't remember ever meeting anyone who produced such a reaction in her. The only other person she'd ever wanted to commit violence to was her ex-husband, John, and that was only after she found out what a no good, lying, cheating, bastard he was.

Perfectly reasonable to want to punch him a time or two.

Rolling over onto her stomach, she studied the oak wood dresser and armoire on either side of the room. This used to be the primary bedroom, but after her uncle had passed away, her aunt transformed his study into her bedroom and their bedroom into a guest room. Was staying in the room they had shared too much for her?

What would it be like to love someone so much? She had loved John, but wouldn't it have hurt more to lose him? The anger of betrayal still churned in her gut, but she didn't miss him. She didn't mourn the loss of her marriage. What did that say about her? Did they just grow apart, or did she just convince herself affection and comfort were love?

She rose and walked over to the window overlooking the front of the house. A flash of movement in her peripheral vision prompted her to look down at the driveway. Sebastian walked to a black, expensive-looking car. Her aunt's lawyer was a markedly good-looking man. Of course, he was probably all too aware of his attraction and used it to his advantage. A man who looked like him couldn't not be aware. Women had probably been throwing themselves at him from the time he left the cradle. His charm and confidence only made him more appealing.

As if sensing her perusal, he suddenly looked straight up at her. He stared for a moment prior to giving her a melting grin and a quick wave before he got in the car.

Cory leaned against the window frame as he drove away. There was something about Sebastian which made her a tad uneasy. Maybe she was becoming too paranoid in questioning everyone's motives, but the way he so completely ignored Finn and how he stared at her as if he was trying to see inside her didn't sit well with Cory. And maybe it was his blatant interest in her. That was probably the reason. The ink was barely dry on the divorce papers, so she wasn't exactly looking to get involved with anyone.

Slipping her phone from the back pocket of her jeans, where she'd stuffed it after grabbing it from her car and darting across the road before Finn took off without her, she dialed her friend, Melanie, to let her know she'd arrived safe and sound.

"It's about time. I was getting worried."

"Sorry Mel, it took me a little longer than I thought." A brief pang squeezed her chest. Melanie was the only thing she missed from New Jersey. Her friendship had been a godsend throughout her husband's infidelity, subsequent divorce, and being laid off from her job in the midst of it all. "Do you remember when we met?"

Melanie's melodic chuckle sounded over the phone. "How could I forget? I arrived to welcome you to the neighborhood with freshly baked cookies, and you dropped a box full of books on my foot, breaking it in two places."

Cory winced. "Oh my gosh, I still feel awful about hurting you." She remembered the startled surprise in Mel's brown eyes being replaced by pain. The two had bonded during the drive to the hospital and the long wait for x-rays and then the cast. "Still the best oatmeal and raisin cookies I've ever had."

"I'll bake some more and send them to you. I wish you weren't so far away. I'm going to miss having you next door."

The thought of her old house didn't bring any wistful feelings of regret. The brick colonial sat smack dab in the center of a neighborhood filled with its carbon copy, like a line of identical English soldiers marching off to battle. The house had been a reflection of her husband, not her, which was why she hadn't fought him over ownership.

"I'm going to miss you too, but I needed a fresh start, and Aunt Addy's invitation to come stay with her came at just the right time. I can help her while I figure out what to do with the rest of my life."

"No chance of getting your old job back?"

"No. They eliminated my position. They're still downsizing. It doesn't look good for the company. Part of me is sad. I feel for all the people in the same boat as me. I started there as an intern in college."

After ten years of demanding work and long hours, they hadn't given her the courtesy of telling her in person, but instead sent her a short message stating she was being let go because of economic downturns. "The other part of me is still angry. They let me go in a damn email after all."

Cory traced the frame of the window with her fingertip. "I hate the thought I've become a cliché. A divorcee of a husband who cheated on her with his secretary, and now I'm at a loss with what to do with my life."

"Honey, him cheating with his secretary doesn't make you a cliché. It makes him one." Mel sighed. "The universe certainly gave you a push, didn't it?"

"More like a swift kick in the pants."

Mel's laughter rang loud and true before trickling off. "Promise we'll keep in touch, okay?"

"Always, we'll talk soon." Cory hung up and stared out the window of her new home.

Finn's dark head appeared in view, and Cory immediately took a step back. She didn't want to be caught looking at him, but she couldn't resist peeking out the window from a distance. His long-legged stride reached the car quickly, and unlike Sebastian, he didn't look up before getting in the car and driving away.

She leaned forward, wanting to see which of the houses was his, but he didn't stop at any of them. He roared off down the street and out of sight. Cory frowned and stepped closer to the window. He had said it was a client's car, so maybe he needed to return it. So, which house was his? There was the blue colonial across the street, a small brick ranch on the right, or perhaps it could be one of the other houses farther down the street out of view. Some people used the word neighbor loosely.

Oh, who cares which house is his? It would be best to avoid that man. She and Finn were like oil and water. Shaking her head at herself, she walked back over to the bed and sat down. Hanging her head, she groaned in dismay.

Damn it, she was going to have to talk to him, and soon.

Her luggage was in her car.

Chapter Two

Following the sounds of clanking pots and running water emanating from the back of the house, Cory entered the kitchen and smiled. Her aunt hummed as she prepared dinner. "I have particularly fond memories of sitting at the kitchen table and watching you make some yummy treats."

Aunt Addy gave a small start and touched her chest as she faced the doorway. "Oh Coralea, I didn't hear you."

"I'm sorry. I didn't mean to startle you."

She dismissed it with a wave of her hand and smiled. "It's nothing. You didn't want to rest, dear?"

"I'm actually not tired in the least. I feel quite energized, actually. Besides, I thought I was here to be of help to you, not lie about. What are you making, and what can I do to help?

"I'm making some chicken parmigiana. If I remember correctly, it was one of your favorites?"

"Most definitely. I still remember the first time you cooked it for me. I had decided I would never eat meat again after I discovered where it came from, and then I took a bite of the chicken parmesan, thinking it was just pasta. It was too late once I realized there was meat in the dish. The scrumptious taste made it pretty clear I would never make it as a vegetarian."

Aunt Addy stirred the sauce on the stove. "I'd forgotten about that." She smiled at Cory and waved a hand in the table's direction in the corner across from the back door. "You being here is already a comfort to me, and the day I can't cook a meal in my kitchen is the day they might as well take me away. Go sit at the table like you used to do, and we can catch up."

Cory sat down at the old, scarred, pine table while her aunt traveled efficiently between the fridge, counter, and stove. The warmth from the oven and the scent of Italian seasonings from the sauce permeated the room.

Her aunt looked over at her and smiled once again. "So, tell me, what do you think of Finnegan and Sebastian?"

"Um, well, they both seem to care a great deal about you."

"They've both been indispensably helpful in their own ways. Sweet boys."

Sweet boys? Not how she would describe them. More like two alpha males, confident their way is the right way and the rest of the world needs to fall in line. Maybe she was being too harsh, but the male gender hadn't been showing themselves to her in the best light lately. A deep sigh welled within her. If she wasn't careful, she would turn into a seriously bitter woman, and that was not something she wanted to do. A few hard knocks would not define her and her future.

She forced a smile on her lips. "I'm glad you've had them to help you. I'm sorry I haven't been here for you, Aunt Addy."

Cory's aunt paused over the cutting board where she had been cutting vegetables. She set the knife down and wiped her hands on her sunny yellow apron. Taking the seat across from her, she reached out and took her hand. "Coralea, I don't want you to feel one drop of guilt or obligation toward me. I'm a grown woman and more than capable of taking care of myself. The things I can no longer do...well I can hire someone to do them. Between what my parents left me and what your uncle and I saved over the years, I am extremely comfortable. Do you think for one moment I would want or expect you or your mother to put your lives on hold to come take care of me? I asked you here because I thought it might be a desirable choice for you right now while your life is changing so much." A warm smile plumped her cheeks and created a sheen to her eyes. "And, yes, selfishly, I've missed you and want to spend time with you."

Cory gently squeezed her aunt's hand. "When Mother mentioned you wanted me to come for a visit, I grabbed for it like the lifeline it is. I always felt such a sense of comfort here with you, and that is something I need more desperately than I thought. I'm a bit out of sorts these days. I need to start over with my life, and it feels rather daunting. I don't have a clue where to start."

After a quick pat to their joined hands, Aunt Addy stood and made her way back to the counter. "Well, now, I'd say you've already made an excellent start. You got rid of that no-good scoundrel of a husband and you relocated here where you can take all the time you need to figure out what next steps you want to take."

"Thank you, Aunt Addy."

Her aunt seasoned and coated the chicken. Memories of watching her do the same steps years ago superimposed on the scene. The same dark cabinets with the white porcelain pulls. The same fruit accented wallpaper. Her summer breaks and holidays as a child had been spent here. What she had told her aunt was the truth, this place and her aunt generated a sense of comfort and welcome. No expectations, no disappointment, just acceptance.

After placing the pan in the oven, Aunt Addy returned to her seat at the table. "Now dinner is going to take a while, so it's the perfect time to talk. There are some things we should discuss."

"Of course. What do you want to talk about?"

She folded her hands in her lap and stared out the window. "Well, there is the matter of my will which Sebastian has been handling for me. It hasn't really changed since Albert passed away eighteen years ago, but I thought it best to update and make sure everything is in order."

Cory frowned. Her aunt seemed hesitant. Was it talking about wills? Most people became uncomfortable about discussing them, but it might be something more. Did her aunt think she expected to be named in the will? Was she about to tell her she'd left everything to someone else? Well, that was fine with her. It really was. Aunt Addy could leave her estate to whoever she wanted. Except her neighbor maybe, she might have a problem with that. Well, unless she could make sure he wasn't taking advantage of her aunt.

"If there's something you're trying to tell me, I want you to know whatever it is, it's fine. I hope you know you can tell me anything, and it will be okay."

Her aunt's smile seemed a bit forced, but her dainty shoulders straightened a bit more as she appeared to decide. "I've had some health concerns lately. That's why I want to make sure everything is taken care of."

The breath stuttered in Cory's chest, and she hastily blinked back the tears gathering in her eyes. Dear God, please don't let it be serious.

"What sort of health concerns? Mother never mentioned you were ill."

"Well that would be because I haven't told her. I love your mother, but Margaret would immediately try to take over my life. She'd have me installed in her house and every decision about my medical treatment under her jurisdiction. She'd do it out of love of course, but I need my independence, and I can make my own decisions."

"No one knows what my mother is like better than me. I understand your reasoning. Any time I'm at my parents' house, even if it's less than a day, she attempts to run my life again like when I was a kid."

"She means well."

"I know she does. It's her way of showing her love, I think."

Aunt Addy nodded and glanced down at her hands. "It's my heart."

A jolt of alarm stiffened her body. Okay, that could mean a lot of things. No reason to panic, yet.

"What exactly is wrong with your heart? You didn't have a heart attack, did you?" Surely someone would have called the family for that, wouldn't they?

"No, no. I had some warnings, palpitations, shortness of breath, and some pains. Being a doctor's wife for forty years I know when to go to the doctor. He's prescribed some medications and I need to be more careful, but I should be okay. It puts things in perspective though."

Not exactly great news, but it could be much worse. All right, a plan of action—gather the facts and do whatever needs to be done to make sure Aunt Addy stays healthy. "I'd like to go with you to see your doctor if that's all right. I think I should know how to help you and what to look for, don't you? I won't intrude on your independence. I just want to help and be prepared."

Her aunt beamed and leaned over to pat Cory's hand. "I know, dear. I think that might be a good idea. It will give us both peace of mind, I think."

"Good, that's settled."

"Yes, now back to my will. As I said, it hasn't changed since I made it after Albert passed away, but apparently some laws have changed. Sebastian has suggested setting up a trust for tax purposes. You, of course, are still my heir."

Cory opened her mouth and then closed it, not sure what to say.

"Is something wrong, dear?"

"Umm...I guess I'm a little shocked. I never really thought about it, but what about Mother? Shouldn't she be your heir?"

"Margaret and I discussed it when Albert passed away. She understood and agreed with my choice. Your mother has no interest in this house, or any need of my money."

"Oh." Cory's mother was a retired surgeon and her father a lawyer. She knew their finances were in decent shape. She couldn't imagine them wanting to move away from New York either. They were both firmly established and active in their community. Her mother had joined the historical society and had made it her mission to save old buildings and the history they represented. Secretly, she believed her father had suggested the society as a way to keep her mother occupied and not interfere with his own semi-retirement or his golf game.

"Coralea don't think you're under any obligation either. It will be completely up to you what you do with this place when I'm gone. As much as I would love the thought of you making a permanent home here and the house staying in the family for future generations, I'm realistic enough to understand that might not be your want. Whatever you decide is okay."

"I don't know what to say. I feel like I should say thank you, but I really hope this is all a moot point and your will isn't needed for an extremely long, long time." Like several decades.

"Thank you dear, me too. Now there is another matter I do need to discuss with you."

"Okay."

She brushed imaginary crumbs off the table and then clasped her hands together in her lap. A pinched look between her eyes appeared as she stared out the window, which had Cory tensing. What could be more dire than discussing her health and will?

"Aunt Addy?"

"I'm sorry dear, I'm just not sure where to begin, or how to explain."

"You're worrying me here. Is there something else about your health?"

She shook her head and gave a wan smile. "No, it's not about my health. It's family history, really."

Cory leaned back against her chair and waited for her aunt to continue. Visions of possible dark family secrets shuffled through her head. The way her luck was going lately it could be anything. Criminals in the family tree? A body or two buried in the backyard?

"Perhaps it's best if I show it to you." Aunt Addy stood and leaned against her chair for a moment. "I'll be right back." She left the kitchen and headed for her bedroom.

What could it be? Was there some great family secret? What could cause her aunt to be so hesitant about telling her whatever it was she wanted to tell her?

Cory drummed her fingertips on the table. Should she call her mother?

No, she doesn't have enough information to pull that trigger. Mother would give her an exasperated sigh, launch into a lecture of what she should have done differently, and then show up and take over.

She glanced at the clock on the wall. Aunt Addy had been gone for several minutes. Should she go check on her?

The sound of her aunt shuffling back into the kitchen reached her.

Her aunt placed a small wooden chest on the table. The sides were smooth with no markings. Black hinges and a black keyhole were the only decorations. She also set a small old-fashioned key down.

Cory stared at the chest for a moment wondering what could be inside. She looked at her aunt now seated across from her. Aunt Addy stared at the chest with what could only be described as fear. What on earth was in the chest?

"Aunt Addy?"

"You'll probably think of me as a fool."

"Of course, I won't." Cory stretched across the table and gave her aunt's hand a gentle squeeze.

"I feel like one. Here I am, an eighty-seven-year-old woman afraid of a box."

"What's in the box?"

"I don't know," she whispered.

"You don't know? I'm confused."

"I'm sorry dear. I'm really not handling this especially well."

Biting her lip, Cory glanced back and forth between the chest and her aunt. Her aunt sat rigid in her chair. How could she not know what was in it and yet be afraid? Cory had the urge to put the key in the lock and open it herself, but she didn't want to upset her aunt or her heart.

"I stumbled across it while cleaning out my father's things when he passed away. You see, my mother had been ill for some time. She barely left her bed at all, and then my father passed away abruptly from a heart attack. I moved in temporarily with her. The plan was for her to come live with us, so I was sorting through all their belongings. I found the chest in my father's safe. There was no key, so I showed it to my mother and asked if she knew what it was and where the key was."

"When she saw the chest, she made the sign of the cross and told me to get it out of her sight. My mother was a religious woman, but I'd never witnessed her act in such a manner. Naturally, I didn't want to upset her, so I put it back in my father's safe intending to ask his lawyer about it. When I returned to my mother's room, she said it was cursed and made me promise never to speak of it again—to anyone. She was so agitated I had to agree." Aunt Addy plucked a tissue tucked in her sleeve and dabbed at her nose. "She died the next day."

"I'm so sorry that must have been awful for you. But are you saying you think it was the chest?"

She gave her a sad smile. "Not really. My rational brain tells me how ridiculous that is." Aunt Addy smoothed back her hair. "I found the key when I opened my father's safe deposit box."

"You've never been tempted to open it?"

"Oh, I opened it the same day."

Cory rubbed her forehead. "I don't understand. You said you didn't know what's in the box."

"Yes. You see inside the chest is a note and a box. I don't know what is in the box."

"What does the note say?"

"It was written by my father's grandmother. It says the box is cursed and must be protected and kept secret from anyone outside the family."

"That's it? No explanation? Who cursed it and why? It says nothing else?"

Her aunt swallowed audibly. "A list of names and dates of their deaths. There's an engraving on top of the box. It sounds like a curse."

"You think their deaths have something to do with the box?"

Her hand fluttered next to her pale face. "I know how silly this all sounds. I was overly distraught. I had just lost both my parents in a shockingly brief time. My brother Joseph, your grandfather, had died in the war a few years before. It seemed like maybe our family *was* a bit cursed. I felt deeply alone. If it wasn't for Albert, I don't know how I would've made it through."

The events had all happened long before Coralea was born. She'd never met her grandfather. He had died in the Vietnam War. Her mother really never talked about him, or his parents. She did know her aunt was never able to conceive children and had gone through a bit of depression over it.

"I'm sorry. I can't imagine all the loss you've experienced."

"I thought about throwing the box away, but I was afraid to. Afraid something bad would happen. So, I locked it away in a safe deposit box and pretended it didn't exist." She stared at her hands clenched in her lap. "Coralea, I've tried to decide what the right thing to do is. I don't want to transfer this burden to you, or your mother. I think your mother would decree it ridiculous and throw it away. I fear it enough, not to let that happen. It said it must be protected and kept secret. I have done that, but with my health lately I thought it best to tell you all

I know. I didn't want you to find it if something happened to me and have no forewarning."

Cory pondered over the box and her aunt's fearful warnings. She glanced out the window of the back door. The tree branches swayed outside the window. Leaf buds covered the tree and soon shades of green would blanket the branches. Spring was in full swing. A time for new beginnings, wasn't it?

"I respect you and your fear. I can't say I believe in curses though." She looked down at the chest. An urge to pick it up and open it surged within her. "I want to know what's inside. What if it's just a memento and your great grandmother was a bit over dramatic? Didn't people used to be really superstitious? It could all be coincidence."

"It doesn't scare you at all?"

"Honestly? No. I just really want to open it."

"All right, it's your decision now. Maybe I am just a silly old woman in a long line of them."

Cory leaned forward earnestly. "Oh no. I don't think you're silly at all. I'm just saying I'd rather know for sure."

"I *would* like to resolve the matter and stop worrying about it." Aunt Addy crossed her legs.

Cory picked up the chest and inserted the key into the lock. It turned with a bit of jiggling, and she lifted the lid. Inside was just as her aunt had said—a folded note stating the box was cursed. Protect it and keep it a family secret. A brief list of names and dates of their death accompanied the note. Didn't some families keep this kind of list in an old family bible or something similar?

She set the note aside and examined the box nestled in a bed of black velvet. Where the chest was exceedingly simple, the box was ornate in comparison. Scroll work surrounded the short verse engraved on the top of the box.

A secret entrusted
A burden shared
My heart and soul bared
Our lives forever ensnared

. . .

OKAY, that didn't really sound like a curse. She didn't know what it meant. It could be anything really, or nothing at all. Cory picked up the box and when her aunt gasped out loud, she almost dropped it. Smiling to reassure her aunt, she once again surveyed the box.

The sides held more scroll work, leaves, and flowers were engraved in an intricate pattern. She tilted the box right and left and lifted it higher to see the bottom. There was no seam. Was there even a way to open it? Maybe it was just a cube of wood someone had decorated. Stories had a way of getting twisted in the retelling. It could be nothing more than a carved hunk of wood an ancestor told a fanciful tale about that got blown out of proportion over the many years.

She gave it a shake. A slight knock could be heard. It sounded like something might be contained within, but how?

"I don't know how to get inside. Are you sure it opens?"

"Well no, I'm not sure. I've told you everything I know."

Cory examined it from every angle and tried pulling each side, but nothing happened. It appeared to be a solid piece of wood. She placed it back in the chest and grinned at her aunt. "Well it looks like it's just a piece of wood someone kept as a memento or something. The verse could mean anything, don't you think?"

Aunt Addy put her face in her hands and shook her head. "Now I really do feel like a fool."

"Please don't. Your great grandmother was obviously afraid for some reason, and her note made everyone since then also afraid of the box."

"Humph. I suppose I should put it back in the safe."

"Actually, do you mind if I keep it for a bit? I'd like to look at the carvings a bit more. It's really quite beautiful, don't you think?"

"It's yours now, Coralea. I still find it disturbing." She rose and stepped over to the stove. "Dinner should be ready soon."

Cory looked down and was surprised to find her fingers tracing the words on the box. The wood felt warm. A tingle danced down her spine. She closed the lid on the chest and locked it tight. "I'll go put it in my room and be right back to help."

Chapter Three

Finn walked naked out of his bathroom. Water glistened among the hairs on his chest before he wiped them away with a dark gray towel. He strode over to the dual windows of his bedroom and finished drying off before tossing the towel in the general direction of the bathroom. The windows were about shoulder height on most people, but on him the bottom sill started just above his abdomen. He was in no danger of exposing his charms to any voyeurs, not that he gave a damn.

He'd bought the single-story ranch a little over three years ago when he'd moved his business here as well. People told him he was crazy to make the move to what they considered the middle of nowhere, but the quietness and space appealed to him. Lucky for him, he had built his reputation enough his clients didn't mind traveling a little extra distance. Working on high end sports cars fed his passion for fast cars. His business catered to the rich, but since moving here the town's residents considered him the new local mechanic and brought him their cars to fix as well. The income accounted for less than five percent of his profits, but he didn't mind. As long as it didn't take away from his bread and butter, he was happy to do it, and it made him feel like a part of the community. Something he was surprised to find he actually wanted.

Resting his arm against the side of the window frame, he stared up at the second story of Addy's house. She had mentioned putting her niece in the bedroom on the left, which meant those two windows now belonged to her.

He couldn't help but smile. Coralea Bishop, what a firecracker. After he got over being pissed off about the near miss, they'd both had because of her reckless driving, he could properly appreciate what a stunning woman she was. Dark red hair, snapping blue eyes, skin like cream, and a body begging for a man's touch. His hardening body reminded him it had been several weeks since he'd had a woman. Thoughts of what it might be like to get Cory in bed drifted through his aroused mind. Would she be a firecracker in bed too?

A soft snort escaped him. She was more likely to punch him rather than allow him to lay a hand on her.

Finn walked to his dresser and grabbed a pair of jeans and a T-shirt. Maybe he should give Joni a call. She was always willing to scratch a mutual itch without any clinging expectations. He headed into the kitchen, but instead of the phone he grabbed a beer out of the fridge.

Joni wasn't the one he wanted.

"Coralea, you have a phone call," her aunt called up the stairs.

Cory frowned. Who would call her on Aunt Addy's phone? Her parents were the only ones who would have that number, but they would call her cell phone. Unless her mother had called to talk to her aunt first?

Her aunt waited at the bottom of the stairs with a smile. "It's a time for new beginnings dear, remember that." She held the phone out to her and then walked away.

Umm...okay, what was that cryptic comment about? "Hello?"

"Hello Coralea. I hope you're settling in at Adelaide's all right?"

Sebastian Marks? She recognized his smooth voice. Why on earth was he calling her? "Yes, thank you. What can I do for you Mr. Marks?"

"You could call me Sebastian."

Cory sat down on the stairs. She had a feeling this was a personal call. "All right, Sebastian, what else can I do for you?"

A warm chuckle danced across the wires. "You could say yes to having dinner with me tomorrow night."

He hadn't wasted any time. "Sebastian, I'm flattered really, but I've just arrived here at my aunt's, and I don't think it's a good idea to desert her so soon. I want to spend more time with her and get situated here first."

"Would it help to know I've already asked Adelaide's permission, and she thought it a wonderful idea?"

That explains the new beginnings comment. She bit her lip and stared at the ceiling. Should she go?

"Was I too presumptuous?"

"Umm...no, I'm just thinking." It's just dinner, right? Not a life commitment for goodness' sake.

"I promise to be on my best behavior," Sebastian stated.

"I'm sure you're always a perfect gentleman, Sebastian." It'd probably be a healthy thing to do. A step in the right direction, and all that. Sebastian was sure to be a charming dinner companion. "Yes, I'd like to have dinner with you."

"Wonderful. I'll pick you up at six o'clock."

"Sounds good."

"Until tomorrow, Coralea."

"Goodbye, Sebastian."

Cory switched off the phone. Had she made a mistake? She'd been here less than a day, should she really be accepting dinner dates already? It would be the first date since her divorce. Oh God, the first date she'd been on in over seven years!

She leaned her head against the wallpaper and closed her eyes. It wasn't like she was afraid to start dating again, but it had been so long. Had dating rules changed?

Good grief, Cory, get a grip. Sebastian struck her as the type who always knew what to say and do. He was a charmer and a gentleman, but if the date progressed poorly, she could always leave. It wouldn't be the end of the world, just a few hours of her time.

Shaking her head over her musings, she rose and climbed the stairs. Really, after what she'd been through over the last several months, a date was nothing to get worked up over.

Still, she planned to give Melanie a call to ask her advice. What did people wear on dates these days?

Crap! She stopped on the stairs and sighed. She still didn't have her suitcases. She would have to call Finn first thing in the morning to see about getting her suitcases out of her car.

Cory took her cell phone out of her pocket and called Melanie again who answered before the first ring ended.

"Cory, I was just about to call you. I need your new address to send you those cookies."

"Great minds think alike."

Melanie laughed. "I assume everything's well. You're settling in, okay?"

Cory snorted. "Never assume, Mel, you make an ass out of you and me."

A beat of silence before Melanie demanded, "What happened?"

"Oh, par for the course lately. I got lost and got in a car accident with an insufferable man, who wouldn't you know it turned out to be my new neighbor. He arranged to have my car towed, but unfortunately my luggage was still in the car. So, I have nothing to wear for my date tomorrow night."

"Wait a minute, you're going out on a date with him? You just called him insufferable, why would you agree to go out with him?"

"Not him!" Cory wandered into her bedroom.

"Oh, then who? You haven't been there twenty-four hours yet."

Cory chuckled. "His name is Sebastian. He's my aunt's lawyer."

"Tall, dark, and handsome I hope?"

"Umm...no, actually that's my neighbor. Sebastian is tall, blond, and handsome."

"So, let me get this straight. You arrived there this morning and you've already met two handsome men and have a date with one tomorrow?"

"I got here this afternoon, actually. Got lost, remember?"

"Very funny. You go girl!"

She sighed and sat on the bed. "Mel, do you know how long it's been since I've been on a date?"

"Well, you were married for five years, dated for almost two before that, right? So, seven or eight?"

"Almost eight. Feels like a lifetime."

"It's just a date, Cory. You go, have a nice meal, hopefully some friendly conversation, and that's all. Unless, of course, it's an incredible dinner with mind- blowing conversation and you decide you want to go back to his place to continue the mind-blowing conversation in the horizontal position."

Cory dropped back on the bed and laughed. "Mind-blowing conversation in the horizontal position, really Mel?"

"Sex, Cory. You remember what that is, right?"

"Hilarious. I do have vague recollections. What about you? Are you still dating your nephew's soccer coach?"

"Unfortunately, yes, somewhat."

"Explain."

"Well, when I mentioned to my sister, I didn't think it was going to work out, she gave me a guilt trip and told me I had to wait until the season ended. I've been putting him off without actually breaking it off."

"Is he such an ass she thinks he'd take it out on your nephew?"

"Maybe not intentionally, but she doesn't want to take any chances, so I'm stuck in limbo. It's not a big deal, just a pain."

"Men are a pain."

"Yes, they are, but some of them have their uses."

Cory laughed again. "I miss you already Mel. What do you say, you want to quit your job, sell your house, and move to Connecticut?"

Melanie chuckled this time. "You never know. The male prospects around here don't seem promising and you've already run into two in less than a day."

"Just one Mel. The other is an annoyance who happens to be nice to look at."

"Wow. I've never known you to take an instant dislike to someone."

"Yeah, well, you haven't met him. The man takes contrary to a new level. Although my aunt seems to adore him."

"Hmm."

"What does that mean?"

"Nothing, just wondering if a little vacay in Connecticut might be just the thing for me."

"You know I'd love to have you, and you'd have the perfect excuse to avoid your soccer coach."

"Well I do want to come see you. Maybe in a couple of weeks after you've settled in." The sound of Melanie fiddling with something sounded over the phone. "Cory, you haven't mentioned John."

Cory got a slight hitch in her chest. "Is there a reason I should?"

"Well, not if you don't want to."

"Have you seen him?"

Mel sighed. "This afternoon. I was getting the mail when he drove home from work."

"Did you talk to him?"

"Not unless you consider his wave, or my giving him the finger talking."

Cory closed her eyes and grinned. "God Mel, I love you."

"Love you too. You're good, right?"

"Yeah, Mel, I'm good. Catch you later, okay?"

"Okay. Take care of yourself and have fun on your date. I'm going to want all the details, so pay attention."

"Will do."

Cory rolled on her side after ending the call. The chest with the box caught her attention. She sat up, plucked it from the nightstand, and opened the chest, then removed the box.

She cradled it in her hands and examined it from every angle. There was no fear, only curiosity. It didn't scare her at all like it did her aunt and previous ancestors. How could one little box scare so many people? She traced the intricate leaf design along the sides. It looked like English ivy if she wasn't mistaken. The sides weren't identical. Which she supposed made sense since given its age it must be hand carved. Strange, it seemed like one leaf was upside down in a different position on each side.

Could it be a puzzle box?

She just needed to figure out the solution.

Cory pressed on the upside-down leaves in different sequences, but nothing happened. There was no give in any of the leaf carvings. She flipped it over and looked at the bottom.

There was a spiral pattern of leaves. She searched each leaf and discovered an upside-down leaf in the very center of the spiral. Placing the tip of her finger on it and exerting a bit of pressure, there was the slightest movement beneath her fingertip. She turned the box right side up and examined it a moment before pushing each upside-down leaf on each side in a clockwise motion.

After pressing the last leaf, there was a small click and the top of the box lifted. She gasped, "I did it!"

She grasped the top and pulled. It wasn't a square edge but followed the pattern of leaves which is why it appeared not to have a seam. Removing the top, she looked inside to find another box. A woodsy scent emanated from the box.

"Okay, a little disappointed it's just another box," she muttered.

It was a smaller version of the outer box with words engraved on the top:

To my line you must be true
With magic alive inside of you

WHAT THE HECK does that mean?

Cory put the box down on the nightstand and put the outer box and chest next to it. One good thing to come out of it, she could show her aunt in the morning it was nothing to be afraid of.

A burning pain lanced the back of her neck. She clasped her hand over it. What the hell? Cory entered the bathroom and moved her hair out of the way. Lifting the magnifying mirror, she used to apply her makeup she adjusted it to see a reflection of her nape in the bathroom mirror. She saw nothing but her red birthmark, but was it larger? It had always been mostly concealed by her hair. Now it showed below her hairline. She'd heard of receding hairlines, but not on a person's neck.

Was it possible for a birthmark to grow bigger? The burning sensation had been fleeting. It was gone, and perhaps she was wrong about her birthmark. She wasn't in the habit of inspecting it or the back of her neck. She had probably tweaked a muscle in her neck trying to figure out the puzzle box.

She wandered over to the window. Darkness had fallen, and the stars were twinkling across the sky. There were no lights to dim the view or the stars' brilliance.

A light turned on in the ranch house next door and drew her gaze.

It was obviously a bedroom because she could see part of the bed. She started to step away because she wasn't a voyeur and didn't want to invade anyone's privacy when suddenly he was just there, standing in front of the window looking up at her.

Well, she knew which house was his now didn't she.

She froze in place, hoping he couldn't really see her from this distance, that he was looking somewhere else.

She spied a smirk on his face. If she could see him so clearly, he could certainly see her. The horror must have shown on her face because he threw his head back and laughed before giving her a two-fingered salute and walking out of view.

Cory groaned and dropped her head into her hands. The heat from her cheeks warmed her fingers. She quickly walked to the bed and threw herself down. Great, just what she needed. Now he thought her some sort of peeping Tom. He was sure to make some snide comments next time she had to speak to him, and if she wanted her luggage back, it would have to be tomorrow. Why couldn't it have been anyone else but him? Why couldn't he have appeared thirty seconds later? She would've already been gone.

She looked over at the box. "Magic, huh? All I've got is bad luck."

Chapter Four

The ancient coffee maker gurgled and steamed as it produced her miracle elixir, drop by precious drop. Cory drummed her fingers on the counter and scowled at the machine. The first thing she would do today was buy a new coffee maker. Glancing down at the borrowed robe she wore, she revised that to perhaps the second thing. All right, maybe third thing, seeing as she didn't have a car.

Staring at the pot which wasn't even half full yet, she changed it back to the very first thing. Thank God for the internet. She would pay an exorbitant price to have it here by tomorrow morning. Yes, she was on a budget since she didn't have any income coming in, but she had savings and her divorce settlement. There were priorities after all, and her morning cup of coffee was one of them.

The doorbell chimed, and Cory closed her eyes in defeat. Her aunt was dressing and couldn't be expected to greet whoever had come to call this early in the morning. She took a deep breath to draw in the rich aroma. It couldn't be helped. She would have to speak to someone before her first cup of coffee. God help the poor soul at the door.

Trudging down the hallway, she cinched the belt on the robe tighter and made sure she was decently covered. She spotted a familiar dark head through the panes of etched glass and stopped dead in her tracks.

Cory seriously considered making a run for her room and pretending she hadn't heard the doorbell, but instead stiffened her spine.

She planned on talking to him this morning anyway about her car and luggage. She just hadn't thought it would be in person while dressed in her aunt's robe, or not having had her morning cup of coffee first. She pasted on as much of a polite smile as she could manage.

"Mr. D'Orsey."

He did a leisurely inspection of her before an annoying glint appeared in his eyes, and a smile danced across his lips. "Ms. Bishop."

Cory took a breath and reminded herself this man was fixing her car, had her much-needed luggage, and was her aunt's friendly neighbor. "What can I do for you?"

He raised an eyebrow, and the smile grew into a full-on smirk. "Now I could come up with a surprising number of answers to that question, but somehow I doubt you would appreciate most of them."

Finn took a step to the side, and she spotted her luggage on the porch. "Thought you might need these."

"You have no idea. Thank you." She reached for one of the suitcases when he stepped in front of them.

"I'll get them. Just hold the door."

After a moment's hesitation, she did as he instructed and stepped out of the way and held the door open. If he wanted to lug her suitcases, she wasn't going to argue.

Instead of setting them down in the foyer like she expected, he continued up the stairs with them. "On the left, right?" He looked back at her over his shoulder briefly with that ever-present smirk of his before continuing up the stairs.

She didn't bother to respond. He knew damn well which bedroom she was in. She marched back to the kitchen. The coffee better be done. Cory sighed in relief when she found the coffee had finally finished percolating. Her unwanted luggage carrier's heavy tread sounded on the stairs and then down the hall as she poured herself a large mug full of coffee.

"Are you going to share that?"

She took the precious first sip before turning to lean against the counter. She took a second, longer sip, the heat spreading through her.

Knowing the caffeine was entering her system created order in her world. She eventually spared him a look over the rim of her cup as she prepared for the third sip.

"Ah, you're one of those. Somehow that doesn't surprise me," he stated.

"One of those?" She grabbed another mug from the cabinet and placed it on the counter in front of the coffee maker. That was the extent of her hospitality at the moment.

He poured himself a cup of coffee and retorted, "A coffee addict. Can't function without it."

"I can function. I choose not to, and those around me learn to appreciate my choice."

Finn chuckled and took a sip from his cup.

Sometime after her fifth or sixth sip of coffee Cory realized just how close Finn stood. A discreet sideways glance showed her she was eye level with his chest. He wore a black V-neck T-shirt. A quick look down confirmed the jeans she had suspected. Her gaze caught on the way the worn denim hugged his thighs.

Heat spread over her face and neck.

"I bet whatever thoughts causing that cute little pinkening of your skin are real interesting. Care to share?"

Cory looked up into his smiling face and lied through her teeth. "I was thinking of my date with Sebastian tonight."

That wiped the smile off his face. He took a drink from his cup while staring at her. "Works fast, doesn't he?"

She shrugged her shoulder and looked away.

"I suppose he's your type."

Cory stiffened and ran her tongue around the inside of her teeth. Did she have a type? She turned and faced him, leaning her hip against the counter. "Exactly what type would that be?"

"You know, all slick charm and polish. Money."

She set her empty mug down and crossed her arms in front of her. "And what makes you think that is my type?"

Setting his mug down next to hers, he leaned back against the counter and crossed his legs at the ankles. "Let's see, you drive a luxury sedan, your luggage has designer labels on it, and most telling, you accepted his invitation, so he must be your type."

The car and luggage were both John's idea, not hers. She had been driving an SUV when they started dating. A year into their marriage he had "surprised" her by turning in her SUV for the car. Not a choice she would have made, but at the time she thought he had done it to make her happy, so she'd gone along with it, and even thanked him. Looking back, it was probably his passive aggressive way of changing her to conform to his tastes.

The few guys she had dated before John consisted of her high school boyfriend, an aspiring musician who ended up becoming an accountant, a brief relationship with a frat boy, and a guy who was more interested in playing video games than spending time with her.

"For the record, the car and luggage were from my ex-husband. Not that it's any of your business. I don't have a type. Not unless you consider requiring basic manners and polite conversation a type."

Finn smiled. "Hey, we're having polite conversation, I did hand deliver your luggage, and I'm fixing your car even though you tried to drive me off the road with it."

Cory narrowed her eyes. "Don't go there." She sighed. "I appreciate you bringing my suitcases over and fixing my car though, thank you."

He chuckled. "My pleasure."

"What is your problem with Sebastian, anyway?"

"What makes you think I have a problem with him?"

She held up her index finger. "One, you two didn't say a word to each other yesterday or acknowledge each other's presence in any way." She added a second finger. "Two, you describe him as slick charm and polish." A third finger joined the first two. "And three, you got a disgusted look on your face when you talked about him."

He shrugged his shoulders. "It's simple. I don't trust him."

"Do you have a reason for not trusting him?"

"Nothing concrete if that's what you're looking for. I don't like how he just showed up out of the blue and suddenly became her lawyer. I don't like how he always seems to undermine her confidence and makes her think she's getting too old and feeble to live alone. All in a concerned way, of course. Like I said, he's slick, and I don't trust him."

Cory bit her lip and looked at her aunt's door. She guessed Aunt Addy would come out any minute. Lowering her voice, she leaned closer. "You think he's up to something? What would he gain?"

Finn sighed and ran a hand through his hair. "Look, like I said, it's nothing concrete. I don't know what his angle is."

"What did you mean he suddenly became her lawyer?"

"She met him when he insisted on putting her groceries in her car for her. She arrived home, and I came over to help her unload them like I do every week, and she tells me about this nice, young man who helped her with her groceries. Next thing I know this same nice, young man is now her lawyer and coming over here on a weekly basis. When I asked her how he ended up her lawyer, she said she liked him and thought it time for a change. When I asked him the same question, he told me my undue interest into Adelaide's financial affairs was duly noted."

Before Cory could reply, her aunt shuffled into the kitchen. "Finnegan, what a pleasant surprise. Have you been here long?"

Finn walked over and kissed her on the cheek. "Not long, Addy. I just brought your niece's luggage over."

Aunt Addy patted his arm. "Oh, you're such a sweet boy. Isn't he Coralea?"

Cory managed a weak smile. No way was she going to agree to calling him a sweet boy. She caught Finn grinning at her over her aunt's head and just managed to stop herself from rolling her eyes. "Well since I now have my things, I'm going to go up and get dressed."

She refilled her mug and walked toward the front of the house when Finn spoke behind her, "Time for me to get to work. I'll see you later Addy."

"Goodbye, Finnegan. Thank you so much for delivering Coralea's luggage."

Cory had made it to the bottom of the stairs but paused on the bottom tread to glance back at him. Manners dictated she thank him one last time. He had gone out of his way to help her. "Thank you again."

Finn rested his arms on the railing and leaned closer to her. "You're welcome." His gaze trailed down to the opening in her robe before coming back up to meet her gaze. "Enjoy your date. I'm sure it will be full of polite conversation and perfect manners."

She gripped the smooth wood banister and glared at him. He gave her a two-finger salute before turning and walking out the door, closing it behind him.

"Like that's a bad thing," she muttered as she climbed the stairs.

"It's a box within a box?" Adelaide sipped her tea and frowned at the boxes Cory had placed on the kitchen table. After showering and dressing in jeans, Cory had carried down the boxes to show her aunt what she'd discovered.

"Yes, it's called a puzzle box. You have to figure out the secret or puzzle to unlock and open them."

"And do you think there's something still inside?"

"Well, obviously I can't be one hundred percent positive, but my gut tells me there is. I just need to figure out the pattern."

Cory picked up the smallest one and studied the rose pattern carved on all sides. "The carvings are really quite beautiful, don't you think? Whoever made these was quite an artist."

Aunt Addy gripped her teacup and frowned at the boxes spread out on the table. "You don't feel uncomfortable about them, or the curse?"

Cradling the wooden container in her palms, Cory glanced at her aunt and then back down at the box. "Not at all. I feel drawn to them rather than repelled. I'm curious to discover its secrets." She studied her aunt's concerned face. Lines of worry were clearly etched in her wrinkled forehead and pinched lips. "I really think the curse was the product of someone's superstitions which got blown out of proportion over the years."

Aunt Addy smiled and rose to place her teacup in the sink. "I must say I feel like a weight has been lifted from my shoulders now that you have the chest and its contents, and I'm happy I haven't transferred a weight to yours."

"Oh no, I'm glad you gave me the box to figure out. It's a mystery for me to solve."

Cory put the box down and stood to walk over to her aunt. "What are your plans for the day? Do you have any errands you'd like me to take care of for you?"

"Actually dear, I have some correspondence I need to catch up on this morning. You are free to take my car if you'd like. I want you to be comfortable here. It's your home for as long as you wish."

Kissing her aunt lightly on the cheek, Cory turned and looked out the window. "Thank you, I do feel comfortable here. Well, if there's nothing you need me to do, I thought I might do some gardening if that's all right.?"

Her aunt clapped her hands together. "Oh, that would be lovely. I remember how you always loved to help me in the gardens when you visited. Did you have lots of flowers at your home in New Jersey?"

Shaking her head, Cory stared out the window and sighed. "No, I didn't. John hired a landscaping service to take care of our yard. It was seriously minimalistic. No flowers. To be fair, our lawn was a fraction of the size of yours, and we both worked a great deal. But my palms are itching to get into your flower beds."

Aunt Addy chuckled and patted her on the arm. "You should find everything you need in the garage. I'm so happy they'll be taken care of. I've been meaning to hire someone, but I never got around to it. With spring advancing, the gardens really need the attention."

"Great, I'll get to it."

Once Cory located a pair of gloves, clippers, and a small garden shovel she carried her tools to the front of the house. Standing back, she took a cursory inspection. The flower beds flanked the brick walkway which stretched from the driveway on the left side of the house to the front door in the middle of the covered porch. She spotted holly bushes, boxwood, juniper, azalea, and hydrangea interspersed along the back of the beds. They needed some trimming, but all in all were in decent shape. The fronts of the beds desperately needed weeding, but it was only April so they weren't too overgrown. Sunny, yellow daffodils poked their heads up between the weeds. Peering closer, she found some lavender and white crocus mixed in.

"Well there's no time like the present," she whispered to herself. Careful not to step on any budding flowers she tiptoed her way to the back of the bed and started clipping the holly bush.

Cory shaped and thinned out the shrubs, before long a small pile of clippings sat on the lawn. The cool morning air had given way to a warm, sunny day, and she had long since removed her sweatshirt and draped it over the porch railing. Stepping back to view her handy work, she wiped the back of her hand against her perspiring brow and smiled.

The feeling of contentment spreading over her was a feeling she hadn't experienced in quite a while. Her job as a project manager had long ago lost its appeal. It had been a job, nothing more. There was no satisfaction or sense of accomplishment. With her future wide open, she wanted to find something she was passionate about. Maybe everything did happen for a reason. Losing her job may have been the final impetus she needed.

Her aunt gingerly stepped out of the front door carrying a glass of ice water. "Coralea come sit for a moment and have a drink. You need to stay hydrated. You've been working so hard out here."

"Just a moment, I want to clear this front section of weeds to see what's growing here."

After clearing away some of the weeds, she found hyacinths and tulips poking their green tops through the mulch. Sitting back on her heels, she called up to her aunt on the porch. "In a week or two, the beds should be sporting some pretty colors."

"Oh good, I was afraid the moles would've gotten to my bulbs."

"They may have gotten some, but I can see quite a few coming up." Cory smiled and climbed the steps as she took off the gloves.

"Thanks." After taking a long drink of the water, she held the perspiring glass against her wrists to cool her down. The chilly water was refreshing. She sat in one of the wooden rocking chairs spread out along the front porch in clusters of two or three.

"Oh my, look at all you've accomplished." Her aunt stood at the top of the stairs surveying Cory's work. "It looks wonderful dear."

"Well, I've got a long way to go, but it's a good start. I'm going to weed next. I'm eager to see what's hiding under there," Cory said with a smile.

Aunt Addy sat down in the rocking chair next to Cory. Her violet dress added to the spring atmosphere. The warm air and gentle breeze bathed Cory's face. She closed her eyes and listened to the various bird songs.

"I must say, I miss working in the gardens. I always found it therapeutic. Anytime Albert and I had a disagreement, I would come out here and play with my plants. Sometimes venting my thoughts to them. They make excellent listeners that way." She smiled at Cory and winked. "They don't talk back and disagree with my opinions. Therefore, I was always right." Setting the chair to a smooth rocking motion, she sighed. "My arthritis gets rather nasty when I attempt it these days."

"I never thought of them that way. I'll have to try it sometime. I do have to agree with you though. I feel astonishingly happy working in the garden."

Her aunt leaned over and patted her hand. "It's in the blood dear."

"What do you mean?"

"You come from a long line of people working the earth. My father had a greenhouse full of plants. Some of my fondest memories are of working with him in the greenhouse. He talked of retiring and starting a small plant business, but with my mother's illness it never happened."

"I didn't know that."

"Oh yes. He even created some new hybrids of his own. I don't think a day passed by when he wasn't working outside or in the greenhouse. He used to tell me stories of his grandparents' farm. He made it sound like a fairy tale. Different crops as far as the eye could see. Lush forests of varying shades of green. He said they could grow anything. Even in times of drought, their farm managed to thrive."

"I guess it is in the blood."

Chapter Five

The frigid, gray blue waters of Long Island Sound lapped at his feet. A small wave surged up onto the secluded beach. Bare toes curled in the sand while the chilly waters swirled around his ankles. He stood legs apart, hands on his hips, and head tilted back, staring out to sea.

Sebastian's cell phone blared out a familiar theme from Psycho. For a second, he considered not answering it, but that could create undesirable consequences.

"Yes?"

"I haven't heard from you," the ravaged voice whispered.

"Been busy."

"Have you located the line's heir yet?"

Sebastian gritted his teeth. "Working on it."

"That's what you said the last time we spoke."

"It's not exactly a simple assignment," he bit out.

"Perhaps you are not up to the task."

He resisted the urge to throw his phone into the ocean. "I'm handling it. I'm close."

Only soft breaths sounded over the line as he waited for the decision.

"Keep me informed." The call ended.

Returning the phone to his pants pocket, he braced his hands on his hips. Anger, frustration, and indecision all warred within his soul.

His gaze focused on the jetty jutting out into the Sound. With a sweep of his arm he sent a surge of power barreling outward. A jumble of small boulders exploded out the side crashing into the sea. Water sprayed up and out. Waves fanned out into gentle ripples.

He gained little satisfaction from the destruction. His wrath centered on another target. A much more elusive one.

Swiveling on the balls of his feet, he strode across the sand to the short set of stairs leading to his modern retreat. A large deck connecting to a two-story wall of glass spread out before him.

Glancing neither right nor left he made his way inside and up the metal stairs to his bedroom. It was time to get ready for his date.

Coralea Bishop had no idea what was coming for her.

AFTER DEBATING over and discarding several outfits, Cory settled on a royal blue jersey wrap dress. She stopped and took the time to stare into the full-length mirror in the corner of her room. She'd used a light hand with her makeup, just to darken her eyes and lashes and add a bit of color to her cheekbones and lips. Her long hair fell in soft, auburn waves over her shoulders. Just a hint of cleavage showed. The dress wasn't too sexy for a first date, but not too sedate either. She wanted to look attractive and feel confident, but not look like she was advertising anything or trying too hard. She adjusted and angled the mirror down a bit to see her high heel sandals. They showed off her legs and the new pedicure she'd painstakingly given herself.

Cory bit her lip and stepped back from the mirror. Maybe she should cancel. It was too soon. What was she thinking going out on a date?

Rolling her eyes at herself, she walked over to the bed and sat down. She was making too much of this. A simple dinner with her aunt's spec-tacularly attractive lawyer. The perfect opportunity to form her own opinion about Sebastian's intentions with her aunt. She certainly couldn't rely on Finn's, she didn't know him either, and her first impression wasn't exactly the best.

The chest and boxes on her nightstand caught her gaze. She ambled over and picked up the smallest one and studied the rose pattern. Trying to figure out the secret to opening the box was the distraction she needed to keep herself occupied until Sebastian arrived.

"What's your secret," she whispered as she angled the box in all directions, staring at the design.

Some of the roses were just buds, the rest in varying stages of opening. Was that the answer? The fully opened roses, like opening the box?

There were seven fully bloomed roses. One on each side, except the bottom where there were two. Cory pressed against the opened blooms one at a time in different orders, but nothing happened. The possibilities were too numerous to keep track of in her head. She should probably write the orders down as she tried them.

She lost track of time as she tried each combination and recorded them as she progressed along. Holding the box in one hand, she wrote the last one she tried. A tiny bit of give beneath her hand.

Cory froze. She lifted the container to look at the bottom. Her index finger pressed against the two roses at the same time. Applying more pressure, they gave way and she smiled.

She continued to hold the two down and then pushed the one rose on each individual side with her other hand, ending with the one on top.

The side of the box popped open.

She peered in to see another, smaller, carved wooden container. Tilting the rose box, the smaller container slipped into her palm.

Engravings of holly leaves and berries were carved along every surface. Once again, a verse graced the top.

Beware of deception and lies
The ones who covet and steal have spies

"WELL, that's not all hearts and flowers, is it?" Was this why her ancestors whispered of a curse?

The doorbell chimed, giving her a start.

She set the box down and frowned. Her aunt would not like what she'd found, maybe it would be better if she didn't show her until she figured out how to open the entire set.

What's with the cryptic verses, anyway? Why can't it be simple instructions like, push here?

A smile stretched her lips. Because then it wouldn't be interesting, would it? She read the words again. The box was well over a hundred years old. Recalling the list of names and dates, she estimated it was probably closer to two hundred. Any bad guys the box referred to are long gone.

"Coralea? Sebastian is here."

Cory did a quick check in the mirror before walking down the stairs to greet Sebastian and her aunt at the bottom. "Hello," she said with a forced smile. Her stomach was suddenly doing a nervous dance prompting her desire to bolt.

Sebastian stepped forward to take her hand as she stepped on the bottom tread. "You look beautiful Coralea."

She avoided his stare and murmured, "Thank you." He wore black pants and a gray dress shirt which fit his lean build perfectly. He must have his clothes tailored.

Aunt Addy stood to the side of the stairs, smiling.

Cory returned her smile and kissed her cheek.

"Have a wonderful time, dear. Sebastian take care of my niece."

"I intend to, Adelaide." He opened the door and stood waiting.

Meeting his gaze, Cory fought the desire to make an excuse and stay home. She straightened her shoulders and walked past him, being careful not to brush up against him. She would not give him the impression this date was going beyond dinner.

He opened the car door for her, and she slid onto the butter soft-gray leather seats, folded her hands in her lap, and stared straight ahead as he shut her door and walked around the front of the car and climbed into the driver's seat.

"Is everything all right, Coralea? You seem a bit tense."

So much for subtlety. "I'm fine, just fine."

Cory sighed and closed her eyes briefly. Between the date and the spooky verse on the box, she'd gotten herself all worked up. She was being ridiculous. This was just dinner, and the box was just a box. "I'm sorry Sebastian. The truth is I'm a little nervous. It's been a long time since I've been on a date."

"Ah, I see. Well, that's a relief. I was afraid I had done something to upset you."

"What could you have possibly done? We just met."

"One never knows what goes on in the mysterious female mind. We simple men try, but your depths terrify us while fascinating us at the same time."

She chuckled and glanced out of the window. "All part of our plan."

The drive to the restaurant was brief, but Cory relaxed and looked forward to the meal. Once he parked the car, Sebastian guided her to the restaurant with his hand gently resting against her lower back. The Tudor style building resembled an old-fashioned inn. The wooden sign proclaimed they had a banquet hall and reception rooms available.

"I've heard they have excellent food here, but I have to confess I've yet to sample it myself. So please don't judge me too harshly if it falls short."

"I'm sure it will be delicious, but if not, I promise not to hold it against you." She peeked at him beneath her lashes. "Not too much anyway."

The interior's dark wood paneling, atmospheric lighting, upholstered settees, and the vases of flowers scattered throughout the room all combined for a welcoming vibe. The hostess led them to a quiet table for two in the corner with a large window that overlooked a charming brook.

After ordering a bottle of wine, Sebastian settled back in his chair and smiled. "So Coralea, tell me something about yourself."

Cory opened the linen napkin and smoothed it over her lap. "Well, in a nutshell, I'm an unemployed, recent divorcee, who has moved to a new state to live with her great aunt and figure out what to do with the rest of her life. How about you?"

"I'm a single, employed lawyer, who doesn't have a plan for the rest of his life and frankly doesn't see the need for one. Now tell me something that interests you. What do you enjoy doing just for you, not for anyone else, not for financial gain?"

Cory thanked the waiter for the glass of white wine and took a small sip as she pondered his question. She waited until the waiter left with their dinner order. "I don't really have any hobbies, so it's difficult to answer. Until recently, I worked incredibly long hours, so I didn't develop any hobbies. What interests you?"

"I like to swim, but you're not getting off that easy. There must be something you're looking forward to doing now that you have the time."

What did interest her? Was she so boring, there was no answer? She liked to read on occasion or see a funny movie, but she couldn't say she had a genuine passion for either. She could take or leave sports. She had no musical ability, or artistic either. The only thing she'd done lately which had brought her any joy, was gardening. Perhaps there was something after all. "I spent a considerable amount of time today in Aunt Addy's flower beds, and I'm looking forward to making more progress with them tomorrow."

A slow smile spread across his face. "Excellent." He held her gaze as the food was delivered. "I'd say you've found your hobby."

"Yes, I suppose I have."

After sampling her meal, Cory glanced up at Sebastian. "It seems your contacts were accurate."

Sebastian paused, cutting his steak. One blond eyebrow shot up. "My contacts?"

"Whoever told you the food was good here. They were right." The filet mignon melted in her mouth.

"Ah, yes, it seems they were." He resumed cutting his steak. "Adelaide mentioned you're from New York?"

"Originally, most recently New Jersey. And you, did you grow up here?"

"Connecticut is my home. You are an only child, correct?"

"Yes, unfortunately. You?"

"Why unfortunately?"

"It was rather lonely. I often wished for siblings growing up. Do you have any brothers and sisters?"

"Yes, and I can honestly say I wished to be an only child from time to time, but isn't that always the way? You had no cousins to play with, aunts, uncles?"

"Umm, no, both my parents are only children as well. Apparently, we're not all that prolific. Are you the oldest or youngest, or somewhere in between?"

The waiter stopped at their table to check on their meals and inquire about dessert. Sebastian glanced at her over the dessert menu. "Coralea, what tempts you?"

"Nothing for me, thank you. The steak left no room."

"How about we share something, chocolate cake, cheesecake, perhaps?"

"No, I'm quite full, but please order something for yourself."

"Well, I'll take a slice of the chocolate cake, and perhaps you will be tempted to join me."

Cory just smiled in response. She didn't really care for chocolate, so it wouldn't tempt her in the least. With the meal coming to an end she realized she had learned surprisingly little about him. She was running out of time to question him about her aunt. "How did you meet Aunt Addy?"

"It's a small town." The waiter delivered the chocolate cake to the center of the table with two spoons. "Ah, here we are, looks divine, doesn't it? You must try a bite, Coralea."

"Thanks, but I'm not much for chocolate."

The dimple in his cheek deepened. "Isn't that against human nature? How can you not like chocolate?"

"No explanation, I just don't find it appealing."

"You're full of surprises, aren't you, Coralea?" "Sadly no, I'm an open book."

"I wouldn't say that at all. I think there are a wealth of surprises hiding behind those beautiful blue eyes of yours. I look forward to discovering each and every one."

During the ride home, Cory sat stiffly in her seat. Her clenched fingers were aching from holding her purse tightly in her lap. She was confident he would try to kiss her goodnight, and she did not know how to handle it. Should she just stick her hand out as soon as they got home and thank him for the evening? Sebastian was too polite to ignore a less than subtle hint, wasn't he? Perhaps that was too rude. Maybe she should let him kiss her.

He might be a fabulous kisser and she'd be missing out. His motions seemed decidedly controlled and thought out, like he planned every move. He probably had kissing down to an art. Then again, with his spectacular looks he probably didn't have to try all that hard to seduce a woman. Maybe he was an awful kisser, sloppy or quick and hard, or a combination of all three.

What if he didn't even try to kiss her?

Did that mean he'd lost interest or just that he preferred to progress at a slower pace?

"You're remarkably quiet."

"Are you planning to kiss me goodnight?" Oh God please don't let that have been out loud!

An amused chuckle filled the car. "The thought had definitely crossed my mind. Are you in favor or against?"

Cory leaned back against the seat and closed her eyes. She'd obviously lost her mind. How could she have blurted that out? On the other hand, at least she knew he hadn't lost interest. Not that she had decided whether she returned his interest.

"Honestly, I haven't decided."

"Fair enough. What are your arguments against? Perhaps I can assuage some of your reservations, so the outcome is more in my favor."

Still leaning against the seat, she turned her head toward him. "You really are a lawyer, aren't you?"

His gaze met hers briefly before returning to the road. "Was there a doubt?"

"Well there is the scenario where you're a con artist trying to swindle my sweet, elderly aunt." Dodge that Mr. Marks. If you change the subject this time, I'm going to hire someone to run a background check on you first thing in the morning.

Sebastian eased the car over to the side of the road and parked.

She tensed in her seat and looked around at the darkened street and woods surrounding the car. If he planned to kill her to get her out of the way, she was going to be really pissed off. She wished she'd worn flats instead of the sexy heels which were now pinching her feet. If she needed to make a run for it, she'd definitely have to go barefoot. Not that there appeared to be anywhere to run to.

One hand was still on the wheel and the other on the gear shift, when he turned his head to stare at her. "I don't have copies of my diplomas from Yale, or Harvard Law on me, but I could show them to you if you'd like to come to my office. Of course, if I was really a con artist, I'd probably have the wherewithal to make decent copies. So, what do you propose I do to convince you of my authenticity?"

Cory studied his tight jaw and compressed lips, and then his hazel eyes staring daggers at her. He was decidedly angry, but why? Because he was offended, or because he was found out?

"Tell me Sebastian. If your elderly aunt suddenly switched lawyers after decades of using the same firm, and that same lawyer had her change her will and God only knows what else, wouldn't you be concerned?"

He took a deep breath and frowned. "Point taken." Shifting in his seat, he used the door as a backrest.

"Very well, Coralea, what can I do to relieve your mind?"

Mimicking his posture, she leaned back against the passenger door and crossed her arms over her chest.

"How did you become Aunt Addy's lawyer and why?"

"Did you ask Adelaide these questions?"

"Not yet, I didn't want to upset her. Why?"

"For the same reason. I care a great deal about her, and I don't want her unduly upset."

Did he know about her heart issues? Probably, he was her lawyer after all, but she would not bring it up just in case.

"I met Adelaide at the grocery store. In the parking lot actually. I saw her unloading her shopping cart and simply assisted her. The next time I bumped into her in town she stopped to say hello, and we ended up having lunch. Over the course of that lunch, she learned I was a lawyer and started asking me questions about her will and estate. After answering those questions, she asked me to represent her. End of story."

The explanation sounded simple, straightforward, and plausible. She had no way to be sure, so she would do some discreet investigating just to make certain he was on the up and up. An internet search for starters and some casual questions to Aunt Addy. Maybe that box and its cryptic warning made her overly paranoid, but it fell to her to protect her aunt, and that's just what she would do. Although, there was no reason to alienate Sebastian over what very well may be just her paranoia.

"I didn't mean to offend you, Sebastian. I'll apologize if I did. I only have Aunt Addy's best interests in mind, and I want to make sure no one is taking advantage of her."

"Perhaps my pride was a bit bruised, but no apology is necessary. After all, we both want to protect Adelaide, do we not?"

Cory fiddled with the clasp on her purse. "Of course."

Sebastian suddenly grinned. "Now was that the only reservation you had to kissing me, or is there another dragon I need to slay?"

She couldn't help but laugh, as she was sure he intended.

Putting the car in drive, he continued the journey home. She stared at his profile a moment before turning forward herself. Did she have any other reservations? He was an exceedingly attractive man. They shared an enjoyable dinner together. Yet, she still knew remarkably little about him, but this was only their first date so that wasn't really a valid argument. An uncommonly long time had passed since she'd been kissed, and she was nervous about it, but a kiss was just a kiss after all.

Unless she made it more than that by debating it to death.

"No other reservations," she stated as he drove into the driveway and parked.

Cory sensed his gaze on her but refused to look at him. She opened the door and hopped out, and then forced herself to stand still a moment and take a deep breath as he exited the car and walked around the front of the vehicle.

"For a moment, I thought you were going to make a run for it. Are you sure you don't have any other reservations?"

He stood less than a foot away from her, smiling his megawatt smile.

"I guess my adolescent nerves decided to make a reappearance, but I think my adult ones have beat them back into submission for now."

Sebastian chuckled, then he raised his hand and tucked a lock of hair behind her ear. "You have an interesting way with words, Coralea." His warm hand cupped her head with his thumb stroking softly along her jaw.

The warmth of his breath fanned against her cheek as he leaned in and brushed his lips against hers, once, twice, and then settled in on the third.

It wasn't sloppy or hard, it was soft as a whisper.

He lifted his other hand to cup her cheek while he deepened the kiss.

Sebastian's tongue tangled with hers as his fingers delved into her hair, angling her head closer.

Cory placed her palms flat against his chest, not sure whether to shove him away, or yank him closer. A second of clarity had her exerting the slightest pressure on his chest. He took the subtle hint and eased back from the embrace with a series of kisses against her lips and cheek, ending with a last soft kiss against her lips.

His thumbs softly stroked her cheeks before he dropped his hands and stepped back. "That was an exceedingly nice end to a thoroughly pleasant evening."

He placed his hand at her back and guided her up the stairs to the front door. "I hope you will agree to see me again?"

Cory softly smiled as she opened the door. She wasn't sure what to say to him and didn't trust any words that might come out of her mouth just then. With her luck she'd blurt out what an astonishingly good kisser he was.

"Goodnight, Coralea."

"Goodnight, Sebastian."

After locking the door, she removed her heels and walked back to the kitchen to get a drink of water. Her aunt's door was closed, so she assumed she had already retired for the night.

She had planned on calling Melanie to dish about her date, but she hadn't a clue how she felt about it so what could she really say? They had a pleasant evening and he's a great kisser?

That she could see herself slipping into a relationship with him rather easily and how could that be a good idea so soon after her divorce? Especially when she needed to figure out just what she was going to do for work and where she was going to live.

And why couldn't she just enjoy a dinner and kiss without over analyzing it to death?

Entering her room, she dropped onto the bed and closed her eyes. She wasn't going to give this another thought. If he called, she'd decide then if she wanted to go out again. Meanwhile, tomorrow morning she would do a search on the internet to verify what he told her and ease her mind. A good, okay, great kiss would not distract her from making sure he was who he said he was.

Chapter Six

"**S**on of a bitch!" After cutting his hand for the third time in the last hour, Finn tossed his wrench into the open toolbox at his feet and grabbed the rag resting on the fender of the car to wipe some of the grime off his hands. He'd been working on Cory's car all morning, and his temper had risen with each problem he'd discovered. There was nothing major wrong with it, but lack of maintenance had produced plenty of mechanical issues for him to address. The filth coating the engine made it even more difficult and time consuming. Why did people think they could just drive a car day after day and not have it serviced? Then they were always so surprised when something broke, and it ended up costing a ton of money to fix.

"Karl, I'm heading home for a shower and lunch. Be back in about an hour."

"Sure thing boss. You better get that hand looked at."

Finn looked down at the blood dripping from his hand and swore again, "Damn it." He grabbed one of the industrial paper towels out of the box by the vehicle Karl worked on and wrapped it around his hand.

"Listen as soon as you finish with the Jeep, take your lunch. Just flip the sign on the door and lock up. There's nothing too pressing today, and if anyone needs anything they can leave a message."

Karl's guileless brown eyes stared at him from his round, scruffy face. He was the perfect employee for Finn. Nothing much ever ruffled Karl. He came to work, did his job well, and went home to his wife at the end of the day after stopping for a drink with his local buddies. "All right, if you say so."

Finn nodded and walked out the garage door. He'd driven his yellow convertible Mustang to work today, hoping to enjoy the spring weather. Now he wished he'd taken his truck. He was filthy, and the cream-colored seats in the mustang were a bitch to clean. He grabbed a blanket from the trunk and spread it over the seat before climbing in and heading home.

As he drove into his driveway, he spotted Cory working in the back-yard next door. It looked like she was digging a hole, for what he could only imagine. Once he parked in the garage and got out of his car, he took several steps closer to the garage opening ready to give her a piece of his mind about the neglect of her car. He hesitated and changed direction, heading into the house. His hand was bleeding through the towel.

After showering and bandaging his hand, he made himself a ham and swiss sandwich and grabbed a can of soda and headed out to his back deck. He plopped down into the wrought-iron chair and propped his legs up on the railing as he polished off his sandwich and chugged the last of his cold soda. He looked across his lawn to Addy's backyard to see if Cory was still out there.

She knelt on the ground. Her back was to him, so he couldn't see what she was doing. Her hair was up in a ponytail and every time she moved it danced around her shoulders. Her blue shirt rode up exposing the pale skin of her back. Finn became fascinated with watching it inch up each time she leaned forward.

The woman had a shape that made his hands itch to get a hold of her. Long legs and more than a handful on top. He dropped his legs down and stood. Maybe it was time to go over and have a chat with his new neighbor. He smirked in amusement. He couldn't wait to hear her response to his lecture about the proper way to take care of her car.

Cory wiped the perspiration off her forehead with the back of her wrist and sat back on her heels. She'd been working on her aunt's gardens for a solid three days now and had started on the backyard. Gardening was a ton of work, but she couldn't remember when she had enjoyed herself more. She planned on finding a local nursery in the next day or two to get some advice and maybe add a few plants to the beds.

"Making mud pies?"

She glanced back to see an irritating Finn over her shoulder. His damp hair glistened in the sunlight. His mouth was quirked in that ever-present smirk he always had around her.

"Is that a tattoo?" Finn peered at the back of her neck. "Didn't take you for the type. What's it of? A symbol or something?"

Cory pulled her ponytail over the mark. "No, it's just a birthmark." She swiveled to face him and looked up at him looming over her.

His hip was cocked to the side with one hand in his pocket, and the other hanging down by his side. A white bandage caught her eye. "What did you do to your hand? Put it somewhere it didn't belong?"

"It's interesting you brought that up."

Cory rolled her eyes and stood dusting off her knees as she did so. She leaned back against the tulip tree that was the center of the garden she was working on. She couldn't wait to hear what antagonistic remarks he had to say...not.

"Are you aware a car requires routine maintenance? You don't just get it in it every day and drive it into the ground. It needs some TLC every now and again to keep it running in good shape. An oil change, a tune up, fluid check, tire rotation, do any of those things mean anything to you?"

She stared at him wondering if she should bother answering him. Admittedly, car maintenance was not her strong suit. She couldn't remember the last time she had brought it in to be serviced. There had been a lot of other things going on in her life lately.

"After working on your car all morning, I know the answer is a big fat no."

Okay, apparently this was a sore point with him, but wasn't he going a little overboard? "Aren't you being a little dramatic? It's a car."

He stared hard at her for a moment and then pointed his finger at her. "People like you shouldn't own a car. In fact, I have serious reservations about giving you back the car once I'm done with it."

"Oh, for goodness' sake, now you're being ridiculous! It's a car, not a child, and it's mine. You have no right to keep my vehicle. Isn't it your job to fix it? And stop pointing that damn finger at me!"

"This finger? Do you see all these cuts and bandages on my hand? That's from your car. It's as temperamental as its owner. And it's a good thing a car isn't a child. Because then you'd be arrested for neglect."

Cory closed her eyes and tried counting to ten, but all she could picture was a branch hitting Finn on the head. She opened her eyes and blasted him. "You are an idiot!"

Before he could reply, a crack split the air and a branch above them crashed down.

Finn jumped forward, shielding her body with his own and plastering her against the tree.

Cory's eyes widened in shock as she stared at the fallen branch behind him. It was just a coincidence, right? She couldn't have done that. It wasn't possible.

"Are you all right?"

She blinked up at him and tried to focus. "I think so. You?"

"Mm."

Awareness dawned.

His hands were wrapped around her back, holding her body against his from the chest down. His legs caged hers in against the tree. She looked up, ready to tell him to move.

His gaze dropped to her lips before he leaned in and captured them.

Her breath stuttered in her chest.

She raised her arms to shove him away, but her treacherous hands clutched at his arms instead.

There was no gentle persuasion. His mouth devoured hers.

Strong hands pressed against her back, arching her even closer against him.

Her fingers inched over his shoulders. She needed to get even closer.

He palmed her bottom and lifted her against him, so she cradled him against her core. She gasped at the feel of him.

A harsh groan sounded from Finn as he rocked against her.

Cory tore her mouth away and turned her head. "Stop! This is insane."

Heavy breaths fanned her cheek.

"Let me go." She tapped his shoulder before dropping her hands from his body.

As his hands dropped away, she fell back against the tree. Her legs were too shaky to support her.

She spared him a quick glance and blushed. He stood in front of her with his legs braced and hands on his hips. His arousal extremely evident, swelling against the front of his jeans.

"If you're waiting for an apology, forget it. You were just as involved there as I was."

A puff of air escaped her mouth. How did she deal with this? My God, her aunt could've spotted them at any time.

"I'm not waiting for an apology. Did it occur to you Aunt Addy could have walked out the back door, or looked out a window?"

"No, but I'm pretty sure she knows about sex and has probably had it a time or two. Who knows, she may have found herself against this very tree when your great uncle was still alive."

"Oh, for God's sake, please don't put those images in my head. Do you have to be so crass?"

"Sorry, princess, if I insulted your delicate sensibilities. I momentarily forgot you like them slick and polished, don't you? How did your date with Marks go? Did he kiss your hand when he wished you goodnight?"

"That's really none of your business." Cory brushed past him and headed for the house. "Let's just forget this ever happened."

"Yeah, good luck with that, princess."

She closed and locked the door, half afraid he would follow her inside to finish the conversation. Cory spotted him stalking across the yard back to his own yard and let out a sigh of relief as she sagged against the door. What on earth had happened out there?

"Coralea, are you all right?"

Cory looked over to where her aunt stood in the doorway to the kitchen. "Um, yeah."

"You're all flushed dear. You've done too much. Come in and sit down. I'll get you some water."

"Actually, I think I'm going to head straight for the shower and then lie down for a bit, okay?"

"Of course, but take a glass of water with you."

"Okay, I will. Thanks."

She grabbed the glass and climbed the stairs to her room. She took a couple of quick gulps before setting it down on the nightstand next to the boxes, picking the smallest one up.

What had happened with the branch? She had pictured it hitting him and then it fell. What kind of crazy coincidence was that? It couldn't have been her. If she was going to make a branch hit anyone over the head, it would've been her ex-husband. If she had that ability, she would've sent a few branches John's way. Possibly the whole tree, on his car, on his house.

Cory stared down at the box, now opened in her palm. She didn't remember opening it.

A smaller carved wooden container was nestled inside just like the previous ones. On top a verse:

Harm None
Evil cannot be undone

THE BOX FELL from her hands onto the bed, and she slowly backed away. "Well, hell." Rubbing her suddenly chilled arms, she stared at the words carved into the wood. Cory felt a piercing ache on her neck. It disappeared as quickly as it had arrived. She rotated her neck trying to loosen up her muscles as she reread the words.

"I wouldn't really have hurt him. I truly wouldn't. And for pity's sake, I'm talking to a possessed box. Great! Loony bin here I come."

Chapter Seven

Cory spun slowly around in a circle. Her eyes widened, and a grin turned her lips up. A trio of greenhouses radiated out from a generous courtyard with a gurgling fountain in the middle. Plants and bushes of all shapes and sizes were displayed around the courtyard. Benches, pots, and even birdhouses were interspersed among the greenery. "How wonderful," she whispered.

"Thank you. We like to think so."

Cory startled and spotted an older woman with salt and pepper hair chopped off just below her ears smiling at her. Warm, brown eyes and plenty of laugh lines graced her elfin shaped face. She stood next to an oversized peddler's cart that served as the checkout area. "Sorry, I guess I was talking out loud again. Is this your place?"

"Yes, it is, and I do it all the time. I like to talk to the plants, and just between you and me, I think they like it."

Cory laughed and held out her hand. "I'm Cory Bishop, a recent transplant. I'm staying with my great aunt and fixing up her flower beds. She recommended I come here."

Taking her hand, she gave it a quick squeeze. "Oh, how nice, we always like to hear someone recommended us. I'm June Barrows, and my husband Alec and I own the nursery. Who's your aunt?"

"Adelaide Stone."

"Oh, of course. I know Adelaide quite well. She's such a sweet woman, and with such lovely gardens surrounding her old Victorian home. I haven't seen her this season. How is she doing?"

"She's doing well, but the gardening has gotten too much for her, so I volunteered to take over."

"I'm sure she appreciates your help. Is there anything in particular you're looking for?"

"Actually, I'm not entirely sure. I know I want to buy a butterfly bush to go in the area where she has a birdbath. I thought maybe I could wander through the greenhouses a bit and get some ideas."

"Well, you enjoy yourself and if you have any questions at all, just ask. I'm manning the register today because we're shorthanded. Otherwise, I'd love to give you a tour. Alec is working with the perennials to the right and he can answer any questions as well."

"All right, thank you."

"Let the creative juices flow."

Cory grinned again and headed for the greenhouse to the left. Abundant hanging baskets of flowers in a kaleidoscope of colors filled the length of the greenhouse. She took a deep breath of the warm, fragrant air. Pots of assorted sizes were clustered at the entrance. They were filled with creative combinations of flowers and foliage. Plants at various stages of growth covered the tables.

By the time she meandered the entire span of the greenhouse, she had created a pile of plants she wanted to purchase in the center aisle.

"My, my, you must have an ambitious plan."

Cory winced as she faced June. "I might have gotten a little carried away, but I can't seem to help myself. It's like plant heaven here. Those baskets are simply too gorgeous not to hang on Aunt Addy's front porch. Then I thought I would make some planters for the back deck. I haven't even gotten to the other greenhouses yet."

June smiled and rubbed Cory's arm. "You're a woman after my own heart. I lose all track of time when I'm working here. I've got someone to cover the register now, so why don't I give you a tour and then help you decide what you can't live without for today?"

"That sounds great. I think I'd buy one of everything if I wasn't living on my savings right now. Every plant I look at I picture just the place I want to plant it."

"You mentioned you were a transplant. Does that mean you're going to be staying with Adelaide on a permanent basis?"

"For the foreseeable future, yes. I'm at a bit of crossroads in my life, and not a hundred percent sure of anything."

"Who is honey?"

Cory laughed. "Very true."

June walked her through the greenhouses pointing out some suggestions for her gardens. Cory couldn't resist trailing her fingers over leaves and petals. She stopped to smell the fragrant lavender bush. It would make a wonderful addition to the area by the garage.

"Are you looking for a job, Cory?"

"Eventually, I'll have to look. I just don't know what I want to do right now."

"What did you do before?"

"I was a project manager back in New Jersey, but the company downsized and let me go. I also recently divorced. Those two events prompted me to decide it was time for a major lifestyle change. So here I am."

"Well that's quite an upheaval for you. We do have an opening here. It's nothing fancy. You would work with the plants, and also run the register from time to time. It's part-time, and the pay isn't anything to write home about, but you'd get an employee discount."

Cory opened her mouth to politely decline, but then thought why not? She wasn't doing anything else right now. She wasn't even actively looking for a job. She loved working with plants. It would give her an opportunity to learn more while also giving her a discount on the plants she desperately wanted to buy. Maybe this was the direction her life was going to take. And if it wasn't, no harm, no foul.

"You know, I think that's a wonderful idea. I can't think of anything I'd like more."

June grinned from ear to ear. "Fantastic! Come meet Alec and we'll work out all the details. Then we can load up your car with your choices."

She practically skipped as she followed June to the last greenhouse.

This was the right decision. She couldn't wait to tell Aunt Addy and Melanie.

❧ ❧

As she drove farther away from the greenhouse and closer to home, Cory questioned whether she had made the right decision. Should she really be working at the greenhouse instead of looking for a more appropriate permanent job? She eased to the stop sign and bit her lip. Was she procrastinating? Avoiding getting on with her life?

Cory pressed the blue tooth button on her steering wheel "Dial Melanie." Finn had returned her car along with a list of scheduled maintenance it would need and when. He'd added a few further admonishments about the dangers of not caring for her vehicle. She had managed to smile and nod without a single eye roll and had carefully kept her mind blank as he went down his list.

"Hey Cory, how's Connecticut treating you?"

"Hi Mel. I need your sage advice."

"Ooh, okay. Let me channel my inner Buddha." A low hum sounded over the line, and Cory smiled. "Okay, what's up, my friend?"

"Well, I just accepted a job offer."

"That's great! Why don't you sound happy?"

"That's just it. I was happy, but then I started wondering what I was doing. It's a job in a greenhouse making barely over minimum wage. I'm probably being irresponsible. I should be out looking for a career job, not a hobby."

"Hold on, I need to check my phone. I could've sworn Cory Bishop called me and not Dr. Margaret Bishop."

Cory sighed. "Ouch. You're right, I sound like my mother. It's what she'll say to me when she finds out I'm working at a greenhouse. Right before she tells me to come home to New York."

"New York hasn't been home for you in quite a while and last time I checked you were an adult making your own decisions. I thought you'd decided to live your own life and not the one others expected of you.

Cory, your mother is a scary woman, but she loves you and I'm sure she wants what's best for you, whatever you decide that is."

She slowed her car as she drove through town. An enormous white church with a tall steeple gleamed in the afternoon sunlight. A large, white gazebo sat in the center of the town green. People meandered down the sidewalks lining Main Street. The bucolic charm brought a sense of peace.

She took the turn onto the road to her aunt's house as Melanie's words replayed in her head. "I guess I can't help questioning every decision I make these days. I don't want to make a mistake."

"Well then, you're setting yourself up for some major disappointment. Cory, everyone makes mistakes. Personally, if I don't make one daily, I wonder what I'm doing. Some of the most interesting things result from a mistake. Think penicillin."

Cory chuckled. "So, you don't think I should look for a different job?"

"I'm not going to tell you what you should do, only you can decide what's right for you. However, I think you have the perfect opportunity right now to figure out what that is. Your expenses are very low because you're living with your aunt. Experiment a little. Find what makes you happy. The most successful people always say find your passion."

She drove into the driveway and parked the car. "Thanks, Mel. I needed to hear that."

"So, are you going to stick with the job?"

"Yes, I am. I really loved being in the greenhouse, and it felt so right when she offered me the job. I want to do this."

"Good for you, Cory. I'm happy for you. Personally, I have a black thumb, so I'm always amazed by people with gardens. I've killed every plant I've ever owned. I finally gave up for fear the plants would rise up and come after me for their revenge."

Cory's laugh echoed in the car. "When are you going to come for a visit? I'm sure I can find you a plant you can take care of."

"I've even killed a cactus, Cory. I'm a lost cause. However, I think I'm going to put in for some vacation time next month. We'll have to compare schedules and see what's best. I can't wait to meet those two handsome men you've yet to mention today."

"Ugh, don't remind me. I'm swearing off men. I never should have gone out on that date. It's too soon. I've got too many other things to worry about. Tell you what. I'll set you up with him when you come for a visit."

"Oh really? That tells me you're not that into him."

"He's a very good-looking man, and he's charming, but like I said, I need to swear off men."

"What about the neighbor?"

Cory looked over at his house. She hadn't seen much of him since last week and what she labeled the incident.

"Cory?"

"What? Oh, sorry, my mind was wandering."

"Thinking about your neighbor? Does that mean you won't be offering to set me up with him?"

"No, but not for the reason you're implying. It's because I like you too much to do that to you."

"Uh oh, still not getting along?"

"Understatement. Listen I'm back at Aunt Addy's. I'll talk to you later, okay? I want to know when you're coming for a visit. I miss you."

"I miss you too, and I'll figure it out soon. You take care."

"You too."

Cory hung up the phone and frowned as she got out of the car. She hadn't told Melanie about the incident with Finn. She didn't want to make a big deal about it, and she didn't know how to explain it without mentioning the tree and the box and the weird warnings.

The boxes still sat on her nightstand—untouched since that day.

Chapter Eight

The murmur of voices reached her ears as she paused at the bottom of the stairs. She looked down at the tank top and lounge pants she had dragged on after rolling out of bed and then back up the stairs. The proper thing to do would be to go back up and put on something more presentable, but the enticing aroma of coffee drew her to the kitchen. She estimated she could grab a cup of coffee and be back out in less than a minute, not enough time to offend anyone with her attire. Besides her tank had a built-in bra and people certainly wore less in public.

Cory peeked around the doorway. Finn's blue-eyed gaze raked her from head to toe, and he smiled. She rolled her eyes and stalked straight to the coffee machine.

"Oh, good morning, dear. Finnegan stopped by this morning and fixed the back door. It no longer sticks. I'm so lucky he moved in next door."

"Mm-hmm."

She held the coffee up to her face and closed her eyes, inhaling deeply.

"I don't think your niece is ready to converse, Addy. The caffeine hasn't entered her system, yet."

Her aunt laughed and glanced at Cory. "Can I fix you some breakfast, Coralea?"

"No thank you, I just need the coffee. I'll take it upstairs and let you two continue your visit." Cory gave a vague smile in the direction of the kitchen table and started walking to the doorway.

"Oh, come join us, dear. I was just telling Finnegan about your new job at the greenhouse."

Cory eyed the door and fantasized for a second about disappearing upstairs with her coffee, but then she forced a smile on her lips and sat down next to her aunt. She couldn't refuse her aunt and be rude. She sipped the hot liquid and absently listened as her aunt told Finn about the history of her family being connected to the land.

"Are you working today, Coralea?"

"Yes, but not until 11:00. Is there something you need done?"

She patted Cory's hand softly. "Oh no, I plan to putter about the house today. What would you like for dinner tonight? You will be home for dinner?"

"Yes, I should be home a little after five." Home? It felt like home. She was settling in here more easily and much quicker than she had planned. Originally, she had intended it to be a temporary and short visit, but now she could see herself staying here. She loved her aunt and enjoyed her company. She'd found a job she was excited to start and see where it led. With the exception of Melanie, she didn't miss New Jersey at all. "Why don't you let me take care of dinner tonight? You shouldn't have to cook every night."

"Oh, but I enjoy it. It's wonderful to have someone to cook for again. I know cooking isn't your favorite thing, but it brings me pleasure."

"Well, in that case, I won't argue with you. Cooking definitely isn't one of my favorite things, or one of my skills either. I will luxuriate in your wonderful meals and no longer feel guilty."

"Not a cook, huh? Did your husband do all the cooking?"

Cory glared at Finn over the rim of her coffee cup as she took a healthy sip. "As a matter of fact, no. You see there are these things called restaurants that cook the food for you."

Finn smiled. "I have heard of them, but I would think it would get old eating out all the time. Personally, I love a good home cooked meal."

"I'm sure you do. I didn't say we ate out all the time. I can cook. I just don't enjoy it. Besides restaurants also provide this marvelous thing called take out."

The smirk on his face faded into a chuckle. He gave her a silent toast with his coffee mug.

Aunt Addy gave Cory's hand a last pat, and then she slowly levered herself up from the chair using the table. "Can I refill either of your coffee cups?"

Finn stood and lightly grasped her aunt's shoulder. "I'll take care of it, Addy. You sit and rest for a bit."

"Oh, I can't sit in one place too long or my bones think they can lock in place. I need to move, always have. Albert used to say I was his little hummingbird because I was always in motion."

A soft smile graced her face as she started wiping down the counter. Cory stared down into her almost empty coffee mug. What must it feel like to love someone and be loved by the same person for so many decades of your life? To still love them even years after their death.

A tan arm appeared in front of her. He placed his hand on the back of her chair, brushing against the bare skin of her shoulder. Damn, the man's skin ran hot. The lingering warmth of his hand branded her skin. He poured the coffee in silence and remained behind her. Cory murmured, "Thank you."

"How about we sample one of those things called restaurants you mentioned tomorrow night?"

She froze. Did he really just ask her out? She replayed his words in her head. Yup, that sounded like a date. She couldn't possibly say yes. She would probably kill him before the food arrived. So why wasn't she saying no? She glanced up at him hovering over her, fully prepared to decline politely. His face was much closer than she had anticipated. A man really shouldn't have such long, dark eyelashes. It just wasn't fair.

"What a wonderful idea, Finnegan. I have my bridge game tomorrow. Now I won't have to worry about Coralea eating alone."

Cory's gaze shot to her aunt. Did she just accept for her?

"Great, I'll pick you up at six."

Finn opened the back door before she could react. "Wait." Cory lunged up from her chair, opened her mouth, and abruptly closed it again. She looked at her aunt smiling innocently at her from in front of the kitchen sink and back to Finn standing in front of the open door staring at her with one arrogant eyebrow raised. Crap. What could she say? How could she decline and not upset Aunt Addy? She sighed. This was a mistake. "Make it six-fifteen."

He gave a short nod and left. Cory considered running after him and demanding to know what he was up to, but that would cause an even worse scene. Besides going out with him would make her aunt happy. She wouldn't understand that Cory didn't hold him in as high a regard as she did. That was another thing. If this was going to be her home now, then she needed to figure out a way to get along with her neighbor. Instead of a date, she would view it as a sort of negotiation for a peaceful coexistence. If he thought he was going to get lucky, he was sadly mistaken.

THE SHOWER STEAM fogged up the mirror. Cory wiped her hand across the wet glass and stared at her reflection. What was she doing? Getting ready for a date with Finn? She had sworn off dating for a while until she got her head on straight and figured out what she wanted to do with the rest of her life, and yet here she was going out with a man who drove her crazy. She should have said no. Aunt Addy would have understood—maybe. Well she had agreed to go, sort of, but that didn't mean she had to give him what he expected.

After dressing, Cory once again stood in front of the mirror. A pair of old jeans, a comfortable T-shirt, her hair slicked back into a ponytail, and not a trace of makeup on her face. Definitely not what she would term date wear. She smiled. He believed he had manipulated her into going out with him, but she would have the last laugh. Hopefully she would get a decent meal out of it too because after working all day, she was starving.

Cory hesitated over sneakers to finish out her ensemble, but in the end grabbed a pair of comfortable sandals. She wanted to make her point, but she didn't want to feel self-conscious all night. Perhaps some mascara and a touch of tinted lip balm might be in order. Halfway to the bathroom, she stopped. No, she wasn't dressing up for him. Cory was done being manipulated or maneuvered by men.

She grabbed her purse, and went downstairs to wait for him to arrive, lest she be tempted to change again. She paced the length of the dining room and back again. Cory stopped and straightened the silver candlestick holder so it sat squarely in the center of the white tablecloth. She glanced at the china cabinet and then down to her attire. What if he intended to take her somewhere fancy?

A peek out the dining-room window to see if she could catch a glimpse of him to give her a clue proved fruitless. Damn it, it would be just like him to do the unexpected and then her plan to teach him a lesson would backfire.

The grandfather clock in the living room chimed. By the time the sixth chime sounded, she was up the stairs.

A couple of swipes of mascara, a dash of color to her lips, and a pair of earrings dangling from her ears were all she had time for before the doorbell rang. A quick check in the full-length mirror made her hope she could pull off shabby chic in case he went the more formal route.

He didn't.

Well, maybe for him it was. His normal blue jeans were replaced with black. The customarily tight T-shirt was now a blue, button-down shirt opened at the throat. Damn, it matched his eyes.

Eyes that were making a very slow, thorough, perusal of her before meeting her gaze. "Must admit, I thought you might stand me up."

Now why hadn't that occurred to her?

"The thought never crossed my mind. I follow through when I say I'm going to do something. Although, technically I don't think I actually accepted your invitation."

"Sure, you did. You said six-fifteen. That implied acceptance."

Cory rolled her eyes. "We both know if Aunt Addy hadn't been there, I would've said no very clearly."

"Maybe, but then we'd both be left wondering what the two of us together might be like. Personally, I prefer a more direct approach."

Her foot tapped. "Oh really? Maneuvering me into a date is direct? And for the record, I wouldn't be wondering about anything. You and I are not going to get together." Her hand waved back and forth between them. "We can't even be in the same room for a few minutes without arguing."

Finn laughed. "This isn't arguing."

"Oh really, what would you call it?"

He leaned toward her and whispered, "Foreplay."

Mouth slightly agape, Cory stared at him.

"You ready to go?" He jogged down the porch stairs. "I have reservations at the steakhouse. You like steak, right?"

She stood at the door with her hand on the knob. "You're insane, right? Certifiably crazy."

He glanced back at her. "You don't like steak?"

Cory closed her eyes and counted to ten. When she reopened them, he was still standing there watching her with a bit of a smirk on his face. She closed the door and walked down the steps and then past him.

"Love it. As a matter of fact, I sampled the local steakhouse on my date with Sebastien."

She approached the passenger side of his car and looked over her shoulder. He was right behind her. He winked at her and reached past her to open her door. "How do you feel about Italian?"

A laugh bubbled up in her throat. He sauntered around the front of the car and slid into the driver's seat. One thing was certain, the night wouldn't be boring.

In the end, they decided on seafood. He drove her down to the coast, and they arrived at a small restaurant on Long Island Sound. They sat outside at picnic tables shielded from the sun by red and white umbrellas. Once the waitress left with their order, Finn folded his arms on the table and leaned forward. "Tell me one of your happiest memories."

Cory mimicked his move and leaned on the table. "All right, let's see, I was seven. My parents took me on vacation to Mexico. I rode a horse on the beach. I remember trotting through the waves and laughing. I asked for a horse for my next birthday."

"Did you get one?"

"Uh, no. We lived in a suburban community. There wasn't any room for a horse. What about you? What is one of your happiest memories?"

"Buying my first car. I was fifteen. I had been working steadily for a few years by then. Mostly odd jobs: lawn work, construction, and my uncle's garage. I had saved up enough to buy a '78 Camaro from the local junk yard. Didn't run, of course, but I didn't care. Took me over a year to get it running and on the road."

"Do you still have it?"

Finn shook his head. "No, I sold it when I joined the Air Force. Still regret it."

The waitress delivered their drinks while Cory pondered the fact Finn had been in the military. She wouldn't have guessed that.

"Did you serve a long time?"

"No, only a few years. Too many rules and people telling me what to do. I prefer to go my own way."

Cory smiled. "Now that I could have guessed."

He returned her smile before taking a sip of beer. "Worst memory?"

She looked out at the water lapping against the rocky shore. "Coming home from college for summer break to find out my parents had put my dog to sleep before I could say goodbye."

"That's harsh."

"They thought they were saving me the heartache."

"Doesn't look like they succeeded."

"No."

"I've been thinking about getting a dog. Always had them growing up. House feels empty without one."

"Dogs are good companions. They are man's best friend after all."

Finn tipped his beer at her in agreement.

"Your turn. Although this conversation seems a bit depressing."

"You're right, and on that note, let's switch to your most embarrassing moment."

Cory considered pursuing the topic, but the distant look in his eyes changed her mind. "That's an easy one. Walking into my husband's office to find him screwing his secretary."

Dark eyebrows rose and fell. "I would've been pissed, not embarrassed."

"The anger hit me later."

"So, did you maim him? Scar him for life?"

"No, I turned and left without a word."

"Really? No name calling or inventive swearing even? You didn't throw anything? Hit anything?"

"Nope, I got in my car, used my phone to search for divorce attorneys and called one on the way home."

He sat back and nodded.

"What? Why are you nodding?"

"Nothing, just explains a bit."

"Oh, this should be good. Go ahead, enlighten me."

"Simple really. Women generally think their wedding day is one of their best days, but not you. Then I wondered if you would say your divorce was one of your worst memories, but you didn't. Instead you chose it as an embarrassing memory. The fact that you didn't kill the stupid son of a bitch, or at least give him a screaming set down which would be branded into his memory for all eternity speaks volumes. You didn't love him."

The urge to yell at him tightened her chest. The words to tell him he was wrong and didn't know what the hell he was talking about, stuck in her throat.

She gazed out at the water. The sea gulls glided on the wind and dove through the air searching for a tidbit of food. Their cackling call echoing across the water.

Anger hadn't been her first emotion. The hurt hadn't come until later either. She had believed it might have been shock which had consumed her when she opened the door to his office. A kind of numbness which had invaded her to prevent all the other emotions from overwhelming her, and a sense of self- preservation had kicked in to get her out of there without a scene, but it hadn't been.

Relief. She had felt relief.

The waitress placed their dinners in front of them, and they both started eating in silence.

"I was married once." Finn took another bite of his seafood platter before continuing. "It was while I was in the service. Met her at basic. We dated awhile." He shrugged. "Just seemed to be the natural order of things to get married."

"What happened?"

"She sent me a letter about a year later that it wasn't working for her, and she needed someone who was around all the time. She never asked me to leave the Air Force, or said she wanted me to be around all the time. Divorce papers accompanied the letter."

"I'm sorry."

"Don't be. After all was said and done, I realized if I had loved her like I should have to marry her, then I would have fought for her. I would have been torn up over the end of our marriage, but I wasn't. It was just another turn in the road."

Cory swirled a French fry in a puddle of ketchup. "I did love him. I wouldn't have married him if I hadn't. I wasn't one of those girls who always dreamed of her wedding day. I'm not sure when it died, or changed, but you're right. In the end, I felt relief that it was over."

Cory set her half-finished plate at the end of the table. Her appetite was nonexistent. A chill danced over her skin leaving a trail of goose-bumps on her arm. The sun was setting, and the night air turned colder. She rubbed her arms, and Finn signaled the waitress for the check. "Let's get out of here. We can drive down to the park at the end of the bay and get a magnificent view of the sunset."

Bright pink and lavender wove together in a tapestry of color as the sun dipped below the sea. The drive home was mostly done in silence with the occasional inane remark or question thrown in. She answered in monosyllables and with shrugs. Her thoughts centered on the night's revelation. Guilt and sadness weighed on her.

"You coming in for a night cap, or dessert?" He had stopped at the end of his driveway.

She swiveled in her seat and glared in his direction. "You have got to be kidding me!"

A half grin and a shrug accompanied his response, "Can't blame a guy for trying, can you?"

Cory opened the door and got out in the middle of the street. "Thanks for dinner," she called before slamming the door. She stalked to her adjacent driveway. The sounds of him parking his car and the car door opening and closing spurred her up the pathway to the house. So much for making peace with her neighbor.

"Hey, wait a minute." Finn caught up to her and gently took hold of her arm.

She swung around to stare at him with narrowed eyes. "If you think you're getting a kiss goodnight, you are delusional." She yanked her arm free and started walking again.

He kept pace with her. "I've been called worse. Is it negotiable?"

"No."

"How about if I tell you how beautiful you are when you're angry?"

She stopped and glared at him. An urge to growl at him or stomp her foot washed over her.

He chuckled. "I like you much better angry than sad. Night, princess."

Finn strolled across the lawn to his own driveway and got in his car. She stood on the porch, her hands clenched at her sides. His car disappeared into the garage. Her hands loosened, the tension in her shoulders eased away. Her head dropped to her chest as a small smile quirked her mouth.

Damn it. The man's methods may leave a lot to be desired, but she couldn't help but appreciate the results.

Chapter Nine

April drifted into May, and the hot sunny days of June were fast approaching. The days grew longer and busier for Cory. Spring was one of the busiest times of the year at the greenhouse. People arrived in droves to add color to their decks and yards and ask for expert advice. Her hours had been extended, and she had thrown herself into learning every aspect of the business she could. June and Alec had welcomed her enthusiasm and shared passion for plants. She spent many after-work hours with them at the greenhouse or their small cottage on the lake. Aunt Addy often accompanied her to visit with June and Alec.

Cory stood back to admire her handiwork. She had created a small circular garden around her aunt's birdbath in the backyard. Two purple butterfly bushes flanked the birdbath. White and pink lilies bloomed around them. A small circle of evergreen boxwood surrounded it all. A smile blossomed across her face. It looked enchanting.

"You're a hard woman to get ahold of."

The smile faded, and she spun around to see Sebastian sauntering toward her. His blond hair ruffled in the breeze. A small smile etched his lips. He cocked his head to the side as he stopped in front of her. "You don't answer or return my calls. A less confident or persistent man might conclude you were giving me the brush off. I, however, choose to believe there is another explanation."

Cory winced. She had been avoiding him and Finn. Work gave her the perfect excuse—mostly. The couple times Finn had stopped by to visit her aunt she had managed to be elsewhere or occupied. Sebastian had left her four messages, one per week. He had stopped by to visit Aunt Addy as well. Cory had been at work. She should have returned his calls.

"I'm sorry, Sebastian. I've been really busy with work and settling in here. That's no excuse for not returning your calls, however. I apologize for my rudeness."

"Have dinner with me and all will be forgiven."

Cory gave him a slight smile. "I don't think that's a good idea right now. I've decided not to date for the foreseeable future. It's nothing personal."

"Date anyone, or just me?"

Had he heard about her date with Finn? "Anyone."

"Well then, I'll have to change your mind, won't I?" He reached out and clasped her hand in his. A sizzling arc of electricity jumped between them.

Cory yanked her hand away and rubbed it on her shorts. She started to laugh, but his intense stare halted the response.

"That's some case of static electricity," she murmured.

Sebastian placed both hands in his trouser pockets. "Perhaps, or it could be a sign."

"A sign of what?"

"That we are destined to be together, of course. The power of attraction." He leaned toward her slightly. "I, for one, strongly believe in signs. What do you say? Change your mind about having dinner with me?"

Cory smiled. "Sebastian, I didn't take you for someone who believes in whimsical things."

"You might be very surprised at what I believe in. Have dinner with me and find out."

"I'm sorry, but no. I have to stick to my plan on this."

"Very well, but be forewarned, I intend to change your mind."

"And how do you intend to do that?"

He smiled and placed a brief, soft kiss on her cheek. "Persistence and charm."

Cory chuckled. "Sebastian, I'm not playing hard to get. I don't feel I'm ready to date yet."

She couldn't help but be flattered by his attention. It was nice to feel wanted by such an attractive man, but she needed to be single and focus on herself for a while.

"Some things are meant to be, Coralea." He gave her a smile as he turned and walked away.

Cory sighed as he disappeared around the side of the house. A small part of her was pleased he wasn't giving up, but it was only a small part, and not enough to change her mind yet.

The small circular garden drew her focus once again. She smoothed the mulch around the flowers and trailed her fingers over the delicate leaves of the butterfly bushes. It was as perfect as she could make it.

A last look at the flourishing garden before she entered the house generated a warm feeling of contentment. The boxes on her nightstand captured her attention as she walked into her room to wash up.

Clutching her arms around her middle, she walked over and stared down at them nestled in a small cluster together. The fourth box, the smallest, rested in the center.

Cory frowned and shook her head. She was getting as paranoid and superstitious as her aunt and ancestors. A tiny, coincidental accident along with an ominous verse and she was ready to believe in curses.

No, she wasn't. She was an intelligent, rational adult. Dropping her hands to her sides, she took a deep breath and then rolled her eyes at her antics. Talk about over-dramatization.

She snatched up the smallest box and gripped it in her hand. Small grape clusters linked by vines embellished the wooden box on all sides. Pressing randomly along the etchings produced no results. She stopped and stared at the carvings for a moment trying to discern a pattern. Counting the grapes in each cluster she noticed each was different. The clusters ranged from as little as three grapes, all the way up to nine, with every number in between represented. Cory began pushing on each group of varying sizes, but they didn't budge. She tried different sequences all to no avail.

Setting it back down she entered the bathroom and washed up. Returning, she picked it up again. She plopped down on the bed, staring at the box cradled in her palms. There was a pattern she just needed to search hard enough.

Twisting to lie on her stomach, she placed the box on the bed and rested her chin on her folded hands. Her gaze traced each cluster and followed every vine linking them. Periodically she would turn the box and examine another side.

Cory got up and grabbed paper and pen and recorded how many of each number was represented.

There were three groups each of three, six, and nine. The other numbers appeared random. She concentrated on different sequences of the multiples of three. She pressed each group of three, then six, and finally nine.

A soft gasp slipped from her lips. The box opened.

A small tingle of disappointment speared inside her.

Another box rested inside. Although she had expected it, she had still hoped for a culmination of the puzzle boxes. An explanation or prize.

She sat up and removed the inner box, which fit easily in her palm. Cory peered at the carvings. Oak leaves covered the entire cube.

Feed Your Power
Never Cower

THE WORDS WERE ETCHED inside leaves on one side of the box. She touched each word. And what was that supposed to mean?

Absently, Cory rubbed the back of her neck with her opposite hand. When she realized what she was doing, she went into the bathroom and inspected the area around her birthmark. She leaned closer and peered into the mirror and angled the magnifying mirror to get a better look.

Finn had asked if it was some sort of symbol when he thought it was a tattoo. It resembled an intentional shape rather than the abstract birthmark she always thought it to be. She studied it and traced the shape with her fingers. A round top resting on a column. It almost looked like a tree. Cory shook her head at her fanciful imaginings and left the bathroom. It reminded her of lying on her back in the grass as a child and staring at the sky fantasizing the clouds were in the shapes of unicorns and dragons.

She wandered back to her bed and sat down to pick up the latest box from where she'd left it on her pillow. Feed your power? What power, and what could you possibly feed it? Wouldn't it just be her luck if her ancestor had orchestrated these puzzle boxes to play a prank on a sibling or something? Although, it would be quite an elaborate charade. The craftsmanship alone must have taken a great deal of time and energy.

Clutching the small box in her hand, she stood up and put the outer box on the nightstand with the others. She arranged the four boxes from largest to smallest in a row. She was about to place the fifth when movement outside the window drew her gaze.

Finn was in his backyard. He laughed at someone or something out of her view. The rear window only allowed her to see a small corner of his backyard. A quick glance at her side window had her frowning. That window provided a view of his house, but not the backyard. She shook her head. Why did she care what he did, or who he did it with?

She turned away, but he suddenly lunged forward. Leaning closer, she bumped her nose against the glass trying to see what he was doing.

A puppy. He was playing with a small, black puppy. A smile crept upon her lips as Finn bent and picked the puppy up to cuddle it against his chest.

He suddenly looked up.

Cory stumbled against the nightstand, knocking over her jade plant, and dropping the small box into the soil.

"Damn it," she muttered.

A peek out the window captured him laughing and lifting his free hand in a wave. She returned his brief wave and bent to clean up the mess. She would buy blackout shades and curtains and never look out either window facing his property again.

Righting the plant, she packed the soil back into the pot, and then lifted the box to dust it off. The dirt was trapped in the nooks and crannies of the oak leaves. Cory used her fingernail to dig it out. As she pried the soil loose, she peered closely at the design. Between the set of leaves an outline of an acorn emerged. She pressed down on the shape and felt it shift. Spotting the shape of two more acorns nestled in the leaves, she pushed down on them as well.

The box creaked slowly open.

There wasn't another box. An emerald, green gem set in a delicate gold filigree design was cushioned by thick fabric. Cory hesitantly touched the brooch.

A jolt vibrated through her fingers, speeding up her arm.

A startled cry escaped her, and she snatched her hand away. She put the box down next to the others and backed away.

Okay, there's a perfectly logical explanation for that. I'm not going to overreact. Static electricity. Happens all the time. Nothing peculiar or scary about that at all.

Cory cleaned up the rest of the mess while keeping an eye on the boxes the entire time, careful not to touch them.

All right, she was a bit spooked. She couldn't deny it. She needed some perspective, and some space.

THE BACK DOOR OPENED, and Aunt Addy's snow-white head appeared followed by her smiling face as she spotted Cory sitting at the kitchen table.

"Coralea, you're home."

Cory smiled and stood to help her aunt with the bag she carried in. "Yes, I stayed home to finish the bird bath garden. Did you see it?"

Her aunt peered out the window of the back door. "Oh, no, I didn't. I was so focused on getting inside once I saw your car, I didn't notice anything. But I want to see it now. Will you show it to me?"

"Of course." Cory placed the bag on the counter and followed her aunt out to the backyard. "I thought you were visiting your friend. You went grocery shopping?"

"Oh, I visited Mary, and she had made this wonderful strawberry rhubarb pie. So, I had to stop by the farmer's market in order to make my own. We can have it for dessert." Aunt Addy paused and touched Cory's hand. "Will you be here for dinner, or do you have plans?"

"No plans. I'll be here."

"You sure? Sebastian asks about you every time I talk to him. You could invite him to dinner if you'd like."

"That's okay, he actually stopped by this morning. I explained to him I don't want to date right now. I want to focus on just being me and figuring out what I want without adding a man to the mix."

Her aunt patted her hand and then continued to the garden. "That's fine dear, but if you change your mind, you know you can always invite someone over. I can make myself scarce too, if need be."

Cory laughed. "Thank you, but that won't be necessary."

"Oh, look at what you've done. It's beautiful, Coralea, simply beautiful, like a little fairy garden."

"I'm glad you like it. It ended up exactly like I pictured."

"It's wonderful. You really have the gift, dear."

"It makes me happy, and I think I have found my calling. Not sure how to make it into a career yet, but I'm working on a plan."

Her aunt looped her arm around Cory's. "You will, you will."

After admiring the garden for a moment, Cory escorted her aunt back into the house. Aunt Addy unpacked the berries and rhubarb while Cory cleaned up her dishes from her lunch.

"Aunt Addy?"

She faced her with a smile. "Yes, dear?" "I opened all the boxes."

Her aunt placed a palm on her chest. "Oh my, was there anything inside?"

"Actually yes, just a moment, I'll go get it."

Cory jogged upstairs to her room. She hesitated for a moment before picking up the box with the brooch and carrying it back downstairs. Aunt Addy was sitting at the table when she returned.

"This was inside the smallest box." She placed it on the table in front of her aunt.

Aunt Addy extended a hand toward it, but then dropped it back to her lap. "I know it's silly, but I am afraid to touch it. Too many years of fearing the box, I suppose. It really is quite beautiful though."

"Should we have it appraised? It might be worth something. Whoever hid it in the box might've done it for security."

"I suppose so. Well, it's your decision. It belongs to you. I'm happy the mystery of the box has been solved. To think so many of us were afraid of it for so many years."

Cory opened her mouth to speak, but then closed it again. To her mind, there was still a bit of mystery to be solved. She wanted to know who had put it in the boxes, and why. Why the cryptic phrases? And what had she felt when she touched it?

"I think there are still questions to be answered. I want to know whom it belonged to, and why they put it in the boxes. Don't you?"

After a last glance at the brooch, her aunt levered herself up from the table. "Actually dear, I still feel an aversion to it. I am compelled to lock it away for some reason. I guess my mother's fear of it is fully ingrained in me. Silly, I know."

"It's not silly."

Aunt Addy wandered about the kitchen. Cory stared at the brooch. She didn't feel an aversion. In fact, she wanted to pick it up. Her fingers tingled to touch it again. Her brain, however, remembered the last time she touched it, and rebelled against doing so again.

This was silly. It's just a piece of jewelry. She needed to prove it to her aunt and herself, but perhaps she would do it in the privacy of her room. She didn't think it was a good idea to yelp, like a wounded animal, in front of her aunt if it jolted her again. That was sure to cement Aunt Addy's foreboding about the box.

She picked up the box and stood up. "I'm going to go upstairs and do some research on the internet. Maybe I can find a reference to the brooch or the puzzle boxes, or anything connected to our family. I'll be down to help with dinner when it's time, okay?"

"Of course, let me know if you find anything. I'm going to start on the pie."

Cory climbed the stairs and walked into her bedroom, closing the door behind her. She sat sideways on her bed with the box on the bedspread in front of her. The longer she procrastinated, the more nervous she got. *This is ridiculous.*

"It's just a piece of jewelry," she whispered and grabbed the brooch before she could change her mind.

The box snapped closed from her abrupt movement. Heat emanated from the brooch clenched in her fist. The words on the box seared in her mind. "Feel your power. Never Cower."

Panicked breaths shook her chest. A tingling vibration built within her palm.

Cory squeezed her hand tighter. She wasn't letting go. There was a simple explanation. She would not be ruled by fear.

The warmth radiated outward from the brooch, encasing her entire body. A pulse of burning heat seared the nape of her neck. The crescendo of vibration culminated in a crackle of release.

Cory's eyes closed as she fainted away.

Chapter Ten

T all trees were encased by an ominous darkness. The slap of feet hitting the earth rose in a staccato of sound. Fear was replaced by resolve. Whispered words of power danced on the wind.

Cory experienced it all in a series of visions. From the first, she understood she witnessed someone else's memories. They weren't her own. It wasn't a dream.

Her body tensed in fear as the woman ran through the woods. The power coursed through her veins. The scene changed. A baby held in arms full of such love coupled with fierce protection. They'd been found.

And finally, the brooch cradled in delicate hands while an enchantment wove around the jewelry. The memories were bound to the brooch along with her formidable magic.

The light mixed with tears as Cory blinked her eyes open. The woman's fear and anguish, and her fierce love for her child left behind a strong well of emotion. She remained still and tried to process what had happened. She looked down at the brooch she still held in her palm. It was no longer hot. It no longer coursed with energy. It was spent. Just a piece of jewelry. As it had been before the woman had used it to pass on her legacy while keeping her family safe. Josephine, her name had been Josephine.

Cory flipped the brooch over in her hand. On the back, the words be safe were etched. She wiped the tears from her cheeks and sat up.

An awareness washed over her. She could feel the power inside her. It filled her and surrounded her like a warm blanket. Energy surged through the air.

She stood and walked over to the full-length mirror, grabbing a mirrored compact from her purse along the way. Moving her hair to the side she examined the nape of her neck. A soft gasp escaped her. Her birthmark was now clearly defined in the shape of a tree. A halo of leaves circled a network of branches emanating from a thick trunk.

Cory turned away from the mirror and approached the jade plant on her nightstand. Tiny threads of light cascaded from its leaves, like microscopic superhighways of energy connecting it to the world.

Touching the tip of her finger to the thick, dark green leaf she laughed out loud as joy encompassed her. The plant stretched toward her finger, and Cory smiled. She cupped the leaves in her palm and watched, entranced, as it brightened and grew before her gaze.

Cory stepped back and gulped. She was a witch!

Chapter Eleven

The stocky, little, black puppy jumped around in a circle desperately trying to catch its own stubby, little tail.

"How delightful! What's his name, Finnegan? Or is it a girl?"

Finn smiled down at Addy. "No, it's a boy. I named him Bat."

"Oh, that's a nice name. Because he's solid black, I suppose."

Before he could reply, Cory drove into the driveway.

"Oh look, Coralea is home."

"And he's off." The puppy raced across the lawn to investigate the new arrival. Finn shook his head and followed suit, not knowing what mischief the dog would get into, or how Cory felt about rambunctious puppies with no boundaries. Although who could resist a puppy?

Cory bent down as the little, black bullet rounded the back corner of her car and captured him in her arms. Bat wiggled all over and licked every inch of her he could reach. Finn couldn't fault the little guy's taste.

"Aren't you the most precious little bundle? Yes, yes, you are."

Finn raised an eyebrow as her words reached him. Ballbuster Bishop had a soft spot for puppies. "I see you've met Bat."

Cory glanced over at him before returning her attention to the black, furry mass in her arms, determined to give her a bath. "You named him Bat?"

"Because he's all black. Hello, dear. Isn't he simply adorable? I've invited Finn for dinner. It should be ready shortly. You two play with Bat a while longer." Aunt Addy disappeared inside.

"What's the real reason?"

Finn grinned. "It's short for Bat Shit Crazy. The dog rolls in and eats the most disgusting things he can find. You would not believe the sheer number of baths I've given him in the week I've had him."

Cory wrinkled her nose and chuckled. "Is that true you little cutie?"

Bat yipped twice and squirmed to get down. She put him on the ground, and he ran off to chase a butterfly around the garden.

The smile widened across her face as she watched the puppy play. Her dark blue eyes twinkled with laughter. Wisps of auburn had escaped the braid holding back her hair and caressed her neck. Her sleeveless, pink blouse skimmed over her curves. His gaze tracked downward to the white shorts topping a fabulous pair of legs.

"Done?"

His gaze finished cataloging her stellar attributes before returning to her frowning face. "For now."

She shook her head and folded her arms across her abdomen.

At least Cory hadn't disappeared inside yet. He counted that as a plus since every time he'd caught a glimpse of her in the past several weeks, she quickly made herself scarce. Also on the plus side, he knew from Addy that Sebastian hadn't captured any more of her attention either. Despite the flowers that had been delivered at least twice that he was aware of. How original was that? She worked in a greenhouse surrounded by flowers. Finn didn't take her for a woman easily impressed or swayed by the standard ploys.

"How's the job going? Addy says you're flourishing."

Cory smiled and met his gaze. "It's going great. I've really learned a lot. I could bore you to tears with all the plant names I've learned."

"That's quite all right, I'm good. Unless you want to discuss it over dinner? We could take turns boring each other with our knowledge. Mine of cars and yours of flowers."

"I don't know how interesting Aunt Addy will find that dinner conversation, but sure. Speaking of which, she said it should be ready shortly so I better go wash up, and it looks like you better go catch Bat before you need to wash him up." She jerked her head in the puppy's direction as she turned to go.

Finn opened his mouth about to correct her deliberate, he was sure, misinterpretation when he glanced over to see his dog making a run for the pile of mulch by the garage.

"That mulch is mixed with manure for fertilizer." Cory chuckled while she sauntered up the stairs to the back door.

"Damn it!" Finn broke into a run after the dog.

CORY LAUGHED OUTRIGHT. Finn carried the wiggling puppy with arms straight out in front of him.

He hadn't beaten him to the mulch pile.

Finn disappeared around the back of his house, and she headed for her bathroom to wash up.

A week had passed since she had unlocked her powers.

She hesitantly tested them at work while no one watched. She was able to make the plants flourish, but so far that had been the extent of her abilities. Power existed inside her, but the knowledge of how to access it, or even if she should, escaped her. Downloading books on witches and spell craft made her feel silly. They also provided little help. There was a lot of craziness out there.

The lingering fear from Josephine's warnings and what had happened with the tree branch made her want to be careful. The danger that had stalked Josephine should be long gone after so many years, but how could she be sure? The incident with Finn made caution a necessity. She never wanted to hurt someone.

Staring at her reflection, she wondered if she looked different. Maybe it was her imagination, or her perception of the world now, but she could see a glow that surrounded her. The aura was faint, but present. Perhaps it was what those who claimed to see auras referred to, but it didn't change color as far as she could tell. The incandescent shimmer remained a steady white, and it didn't change with her moods.

She finished braiding her hair into a thick French braid which covered her birthmark sufficiently. She had since given up wearing her hair in a ponytail to work for fear someone would notice the tree on the back of her neck. She wondered if Josephine had had the same symbol on her nape.

"Coralea? Dinner is ready," Aunt Addy's melodic voice drifted up the stairs.

"Be right there," she called down. Cory jogged down the stairs and walked into the kitchen. Her aunt stood at the stove. "Sorry, I meant to be down earlier to help. What can I do?"

"Oh, don't worry dear. If you could carry this roast to the table that would be helpful. It's a bit heavy, so be careful."

A sharp rap of knuckles knocked on the back door as Cory placed the platter on the table.

Finn stood at the door. How could she have forgotten even for an instant he was coming to dinner?

"Perfect timing. Would you let him in, dear?"

"Of course." She opened the door and waved her arm for him to enter. He winked at her as he brushed past her without a word. The scent of masculine soap tickled her nose, and she took a deep breath while scanning him from head to toe. His hair was damp, from a shower she surmised. Apparently, Bat wasn't the only one affected by his foray into the mulch. "Where's Bat?"

Finn glanced back at her over his shoulder as he bent to kiss her aunt on the cheek. "He's contemplating the errors of his ways."

"He's a puppy."

"Relax princess, I didn't beat him or anything. He's in his crate. I didn't think anyone would appreciate the smell of a wet dog accompanying dinner. Which smells amazing, Addy."

She smiled at him while he took the bowl of vegetables from her and carried it to the table. Cory grabbed the rolls and followed them. "It really does, but then again it always does when you do the cooking."

They filled their plates and started eating.

"Thank you. You know in my younger years I fancied turning this house into a bed-and-breakfast, so I would have more people to cook for."

"Really? I never knew that. Why didn't you?"

"Oh, well, it never seemed the right time, and then it was too late. I suppose if it had been something I really wanted, then I would have pursued it more. Besides, now I have people to cook for and without having strangers in my home."

"Feel free to cook for me anytime. This is one of the best meals I've had."

Her aunt beamed at Finn. "You know you're always welcome, Finnigan. I don't know what I would've done without your help this year."

Finn shrugged. "I haven't done all that much. If you need anything though, let me know. This meal is worth whatever you need."

"You have done a great deal. You're being too modest. You've fixed so many things around the house for me. You've shoveled the snow even when I told you I could hire someone. Mowed my lawn. I could go on, but I can see I'm making you uncomfortable. Just know you have my gratitude."

Cory stared at Finn with widened eyes. His cheekbones held a reddish tint. He was embarrassed. She hadn't realized just how much he'd been helping her aunt. She never saw who mowed the lawn, she had assumed a neighborhood kid or landscaping service was hired to do the job.

"Only takes a few moments more when I'm already taking care of my own. Doesn't make any sense for you to hire someone to do the job."

"I can take over mowing the lawn. I never even thought about doing the chore."

He sliced a frown accompanied by a glare in her direction. "It's no big deal. I've got it."

Okay, sore point. Well if he wanted to mow the lawn, she wasn't going to argue.

"There's lemon meringue pie for dessert. I hope that appeals to you both?" Aunt Addy gazed at them expectantly.

Cory returned her smile. "Of course, though I better not take a second helping of dinner then."

"No worries, I have plenty of room. Anything with pie in the description is appealing to me." Finn added more to his plate.

Cory relaxed back in her seat and absently listened as her aunt and Finn discussed some upcoming town events. She glanced back and forth between the two.

Neither had a glow or aura which she could see. Why did she see one around herself? Could it be because she possessed power? She didn't recall reading anything referencing that in the research she'd been doing.

"What do you think, Coralea?"

"Um, sorry, my mind was wandering. What do I think about what?"

Finn chuckled, and she sent him a narrow-eyed glare.

"There's a town fair this weekend, and I thought it would be nice to go together."

"Of course, that sounds great."

"Wonderful. I think you will really enjoy the festivities. You've been working too hard lately. I know you enjoy your work, but you still need some play time too."

"Going to the fair sounds like fun. I haven't been to one since I was a kid."

Finn stood up and started gathering plates. Before Aunt Addy could stand, he waved her back down. "You cooked, the least I can do is clean up."

Cory helped clear away the dishes. "Does anyone want coffee with the pie?"

"No, but I will have some tea if you don't mind, dear."

She filled the tea kettle and set it on the stove. "Of course not. Finn, what about you?"

"I'll have a coffee if you're making some." He carried the pie to the table while Cory made the coffee and tea.

Her aunt started slicing and serving the pie. "It's not the big fair they do in the fall, but it still has plenty to do. There're various booths people sell their local wares at, rides, and of course, food."

Cory carried over the tea and coffee before taking her seat. "This pie looks delicious."

"It's the recipe I used to win at the pie contest one year at the fair."

Finn took a large bite. "I believe it. You should enter again. I'll be your guinea pig for whatever practice you want to do."

She tittered briefly. "Maybe next year. It's too late to enter this year."

Cory closed her eyes in bliss after tasting the pie. The sweet meringue and lemon custard were the perfect combination of tart and sweet. "You have a gift, Aunt Addy."

"I don't know about that, but I enjoy baking. You must be sure to check out all the baked goods at the fair and bring me something home." Her aunt sipped her tea.

Cory frowned. "Bring you something home? I thought we were going together?"

"Oh no, all that walking around is too much for me. The fair is for young people, like you and Finnegan."

She glanced at Finn. He was busy shoveling pie into his mouth. She looked back to her aunt calmly sipping her tea. Had she agreed to go to the fair with Finn? Had she been manipulated again?

"You and Finnegan will have a lovely time, dear. I'll look forward to hearing all about it when you get home while we enjoy whatever treat you find."

She smiled tightly. "I'm sure Finn would rather go with someone else. There's no reason to go together. I'll pick up a treat for you and me to share."

Her aunt's crestfallen expression made her cringe. She glanced at Finn hoping for some assistance. He met her gaze and smirked.

"I appreciate your consideration, but there's no one else I care to go with. Be happy to escort you."

She curled her toes to prevent herself from kicking him under the table.

"There, I'm glad that's settled." Aunt Addy stood up and carried her cup and plate to the sink.

"I am not going on another date with you," Cory whispered in a harsh tone.

Finn fired back, "Scared?"

Cory glanced behind her at her aunt who seemed oblivious to the undercurrents in the kitchen. She leaned forward again. "Of you? Don't be ridiculous."

"Then what's the problem? We go to the fair together and make Addy happy."

"The problem is I don't want you getting any ideas. I am not dating you."

Finn shrugged. "Message received, princess. Don't call it a date. We'll be two neighbors carpooling to the fair, okay? Stop making such a big deal about it." He stood up and cleared the table.

Damn it. Now she felt like a drama queen. Was she overreacting? As long as he was clear this wasn't a date, what did it matter if they attended together? The fair sounded like fun, and it would make her aunt happy. It would be more fun than going alone. They could be friends.

Couldn't they?

Chapter Twelve

The bright, colorful lights, and the cacophony of sounds transported Cory back to her childhood joy attending a fair. The heavy aroma of fried foods and sweets permeated the air. People milled about sampling the fare, inspecting the goods for sale, or enjoying the thrill of a carnival ride.

Finn had arrived promptly after dinner to escort her to the fair. They chitchatted on the way about fairs they had attended as children and about Aunt Addy's refusal to go. They each had tried to sway her once again before leaving.

The darkening sky provided the perfect backdrop for the strings of lights lining the paths between booths and stalls and the kaleidoscope of lights showcasing the rides.

They wandered down a path peering at the assorted items. Leather goods, paintings, wood carvings, toys, souvenirs, an endless variety just waiting for someone to buy. Cory couldn't help but smile when she stopped to look at a small wooden puppy. "Look, it looks just like Bat."

Finn picked up the wooden carving and smiled. "You're right, it does." He looked at the salesperson. "How much?"

The woman named a price, and Finn plucked bills out of his wallet while the woman wrapped the puppy up and put it in a bag.

As they walked away from the booth, Cory couldn't help but ask, "No haggling? I would've bargained for a lower price. It's expected."

Finn chuckled. "Yeah, I'm sure you would, but it seemed like a fair price to me. How about something to eat?"

"I just ate dinner a little while ago."

"So? There has to be something that tempts you."

Cory pondered that as she looked around. "Fried dough."

"Excellent start. Now are you a purist and want it plain, or do you prefer the toppings?" He spotted a food truck in the next row with a sign for fried dough and grabbed her hand. "This way."

She laughed as she was tugged along. "Does powdered sugar count?"

"Coming up." They reached the truck and stood in line for a moment. Finn glanced down at her with that one eyebrow of his raised. "You're going to share, right?"

"Well, that depends, when you say share does that mean you're going to eat half of it before I can even take a bite?"

"No, we'll split it. I need room to sample everything else."

"I have a feeling I'm going to have a stomachache after this."

"It's all about pacing. We'll have the dough, then a drink, some more shopping, maybe a ride, then we'll pick another food item, and start again."

Cory laughed. "A definite stomachache."

They shared the dough, rode on the Ferris wheel, found a fruit tart and a small painting for Aunt Addy, then shared some fritters. After that, Cory bowed out of any more food. Finn kept going to sample a turkey leg, a fried Oreo, and an ice cream cone with chocolate sprinkles. She shook her head at each addition.

Finn insisted on playing a game and winning her a stuffed dog which vaguely resembled Bat.

Experiencing the fair with Finn was the most fun she could remember having in a long time. Perhaps they could be friends after all.

Other than grabbing her hand that one time, he made no attempt to touch her. He didn't flirt or allude to any intimacy between them. Maybe he no longer had an interest.

This was what she had insisted she wanted. But a tiny tinge of disappointment beat at the edges of her mind. How messed up was that?

Finn stopped and looked down at her. "Anything else you want?"

Cory blinked up at him.

"Another ride? More shopping?"

"Oh, no, I'm good. Bit tired actually."

"Yeah, me too, let's head on home."

They rode home in a comfortable silence. The lights of town gradually disappeared. The darkness occasionally broken with the lights from a house.

Why was she disappointed he wasn't flirting with her? This was Finn after all, she didn't want to date him. Right?

She wasn't so vain she craved every man's attention and mourned its loss if it stopped. So, what was up? They hadn't fought tonight. They'd had a fun time. Friends or neighbors enjoying a platonic evening together. Nothing wrong with that. In fact it was a good thing.

They drove into her aunt's driveway, and Cory tossed an absent smile in his direction as she gathered her things. "Thanks, I had fun."

"See you."

Cory walked to the door. Finn's vehicle's engine revved as he backed down the driveway to the road. By the time she stepped inside and glanced out the window, he had entered his own driveway and disappeared into the garage. She placed the items she bought for Aunt Addy on the kitchen counter. Her aunt's door was closed, and there was no light shining beneath the door, so she was most likely asleep.

Once in her room she couldn't help but glance out the window and watch as the lights next door turned on one by one. When the bedroom light came on, she took a quick step back and darted away. No way was she going to be caught spying on him again.

While she undressed and readied for bed, she wondered if he would ask her out again, and what her answer would be. An instant, hard no didn't manifest, and that worried her. She couldn't fall for Finn. He was all wrong for her.

Wasn't he?

HE STOOD IN THE SHADOWS. The night shrouded his presence. He'd watched as they weaved through the crowds, hands entwined, and followed from a distance as the couple laughed and shared a messy treat together. His phone vibrated in his pocket. He glanced at the screen to identify the caller. A grimace tightened his features.

He answered it silently.

"Report." The broken voice sent a chill down his spine as it always did.

He glanced back at the couple. "There might be a complication."

"Unacceptable. Time is of the essence. Eliminate any complications."

He waited too long to reply. "Understood?"

"Yes."

"Do not fail me." The call was severed. Failure would bring hell down on his head. His conflicted feelings weren't strong enough for personal sacrifice.

Sebastian turned and walked away.

Chapter Thirteen

"Dang, that's one hot looking piece of man candy."

Cory peeked over her friend's shoulder out of the kitchen window. Finn was mowing the lawn, shirtless and in cutoff jeans. His tan body glistened under the sizzling, summer sun. She had no idea he was so ripped. Sure, she had felt the solid length of him that one time, but not how muscular. Granted she'd been distracted by other things.

"I bet your landscaper's client list is all women. Well...probably a few men too."

Cory cleared her throat and stepped back from the window. "He's not the landscaper."

Melanie looked back over her shoulder at her.

"That's Finn, the neighbor."

Melanie opened her mouth to speak, closed it, and glanced back at Finn before turning completely around and leaning against the sink with her arms crossed. "That's the infamous neighbor? How could you turn him down? I don't care how annoying he could be. For a chance to get my hands on that, I could ignore quite a bit."

Cory laughed and shook her head before continuing to put the breakfast dishes in the dishwasher. "Mel, I've really missed you. I'm so glad you are here for a visit. I just wish it was longer than the weekend though."

Melanie had surprised her with a phone call earlier in the week to ask if it was okay to come up for the weekend. Cory had replied whole-heartedly in the affirmative. She'd missed her friend. Phone calls weren't the same as face to face.

Aunt Addy wandered into the kitchen from her bedroom. After sharing breakfast with them, she had gone to get dressed for the day. The whine of the lawnmower prompted her to peer out the window. "Oh, Finnegan is taking care of the lawn. It's so warm today. Coralea, would you fetch him some water?"

"I'll do it." Melanie grabbed a glass and filled it with cold water from the refrigerator.

Cory tried not to smirk as Melanie darted out the door.

"Oh dear, you should go with her and properly introduce them, don't you think?"

She started to reply that Melanie was more than capable of introducing herself, but then changed her mind and followed behind her friend.

"Invite him in to rest too, maybe have a bite to eat," her aunt called out behind her.

Cory approached them slowly with her arms wrapped around her waist. Finn had shut off the mower and smiled down at Melanie before gulping down the glass of water. Melanie stood within inches of him, watching his every move.

"Good morning, Finn. This is my friend, Melanie. She's visiting for the weekend."

Finn spared her a glance before turning back to Melanie. A slow grin spread across his face. "Nice to meet you, Melanie. I appreciate the water. Thanks."

"My pleasure."

"Aunt Addy wants to know if you're hungry or would like to come in and rest."

He didn't take his gaze off Melanie smiling up at him. "Thank her for me, but I want to finish this before it gets any hotter."

"You should come in after you're finished," Melanie practically purred when she spoke to him. She'd witnessed Melanie flirt before and it had always entertained her.

It wasn't entertaining her this time. Her shoulders grew tight. She didn't like it—at all. What the hell was the matter with her? Was she worried about her friend, or was she actually jealous?

"Maybe I can stop by later. I've got some things to take care of first."

"Oh, well, I hope I get to see you again before I leave tomorrow."

"I'll make sure to stop by before then."

Melanie took the glass from him, trailing her fingers over the top of his hand as she did so. "Make sure you do." She smiled and sauntered back to the house, putting an exaggerated sway to her steps.

Cory glanced at Finn. Yup, he was appreciating the view. He met her gaze. "Nice friend you have there, princess."

She wanted to snap 'back off' but managed to bite back the words. Instead she forced a smile. "Thank you for mowing the lawn."

He winked and climbed back on the riding lawn mower. Cory walked back to the house. She didn't hear the mower start, so she glanced over her shoulder. He sat there watching her. When she met his gaze, he smiled and only then did he start the mower.

A slight tingle of pleasure danced up her spine. She squashed it like a bug. Damn it, she would not be happy he checked her out. Especially after he had just done the same to her friend.

Entering the kitchen, the sound of Melanie and her aunt chatting about furniture drifted from the living room. She walked down the hall and peeked in the door.

"Cory, your aunt was just telling me about the antique store in town. Could we go there today?"

"Sure, which one? There's a couple of them aren't there?" She looked at her aunt for confirmation.

"Yes, but I think the one on Main Street is the best choice for what Melanie is looking for. They always have a wide selection of antique baking molds."

"Okay, we'll go and have lunch in town. You'll come with us, won't you?"

Her aunt waved her hand in dismissal. "You should visit with your friend. I can go anytime."

Melanie rested her hand on Aunt Addy's shoulder. "Oh, please come, Cory has no interest in antiques. I've dragged her with me before, and she always wanders outside making me feel rushed."

"Mel, I don't do it to rush you. I just have more interest in what's outside, than inside usually."

Her aunt chuckled. "Well, if you're both sure."

They both answered in unison. "Yes."

A PLAQUE PROCLAIMING, "BUILT IN 1756," was displayed next to the front door of the large, blue, colonial house the antique store occupied. Wide plank floors, small rooms, multiple fireplaces, and low ceilings spanned the lower level. Each of the rooms had a theme of items displayed which corresponded to the room they were once used for.

The front room on the right was decorated with living room items. Twin, tall, wooden bookshelves inhabited one corner of the room. Books were mixed in with various knickknacks. A curio cabinet sat in the opposite corner filled with fragile, porcelain figurines. Antique settees sat back-to-back in the center of the room. An assortment of cast iron implements was displayed around the fireplace.

The dining room held two tables set with antique dishes, glassware, and utensils. Three hutches in the room held more dishes and linens. An antique wooden ladder propped in the corner had lace doilies draped over the rungs.

Melanie peeked in each room, but quickly made her way to the kitchen. She and Aunt Addy began to ooh and ahh over the miscellaneous items offered. Cory trailed behind them into the kitchen, caught a whiff of banana bread and hunted for the source. A burning candle amidst a display of handmade candles gave out the aroma.

An older woman briskly approached them. A navy ankle-length skirt and gray blouse adorned her trim figure.

Aunt Addy turned and greeted her with a smile. "Margie, how are you? This is my niece, Coralea, and her friend, Melanie."

Cory shook the offered hand and smiled. "It's nice to meet you."

The three conversed while Cory meandered from room to room. She traveled the circuit of the lower level and stopped in a room next to the kitchen. Antique tools, lanterns, a few wagon wheels, and even what looked like some antique boat items decorated the walls and tables.

Margie entered the room and stood in the doorway with her hands clasped in front of her. "This is what I refer to as the outside room. Is there anything I can show you, or any questions you might have?"

Cory gave her an absent smile and shook her head. "I'm afraid my aunt and friend are the antique lovers."

"You prefer more modern décor?"

"No, that's not it. I don't prefer any type of décor over another. I never had much interest. As long as it is functional, I'm content."

"Everyone has different interests. What does interest you?"

Stopping to look at a grouping of weathervanes, Cory pondered the answer. "I guess the immediate answer would be plants. I work at The Tulip Tree Greenhouses."

"Oh, of course, I hadn't put it together. You work for June and Alec. June has been raving about you."

Cory smiled. "That's good to hear. They're wonderful people, and I love working there."

"You know, I got these nature drawings the other day from an estate sale. I haven't put them out yet. Care to have a look?"

"If it isn't any trouble."

"None at all. Just a moment." Margie disappeared out of the room. The sound of her treading up the creaky stairs and overhead echoed throughout the old building. Cory regretted the momentary show of interest because now she felt obligated to purchase one.

Margie returned with a handful of pictures of varying sizes. "I plan to frame them, but I haven't had the chance yet." They both looked up as Aunt Addy called from the other room for Margie. "Go ahead and look through them to see if there's anything that appeals to you." She handed them to Cory and left the room to assist the pair.

Cory shifted through the pictures. Various mediums were used to portray trees, flowers, and vegetables. She paused at a watercolor of a giant oak tree. A sense of recognition gripped her, but she didn't know why. She gently searched the front and back for some identification or clue, but there was nothing. Glancing at the rest produced no further clues or the same feeling. Joining everyone in the kitchen, she couldn't help but smile as Margie carefully wrapped Melanie's various purchases.

"Looks like you're buying out the place."

Melanie chuckled. "You laugh, but this is me showing restraint. If my car was bigger, I'd be filling it with furniture too."

"I can always arrange shipping." Margie offered a wide smile as she wrapped the last piece and placed it in a box.

Melanie pursed her lips. "Do you have a card?"

"Of course." Margie handed her a business card as Melanie handed over her credit card. "What do you have there, Coralea?"

"Some plant drawings and paintings." She directed her attention to Margie. "How much for this oak painting?"

Margie walked over and took the remaining pictures from her and tilted her head. "Would twenty-five work for you? If you want me to frame it, it will be more of course."

Cory had some definite ideas about what she wanted for a frame. "Would you take twenty? I'll take it as it is."

"Sold."

Melanie chuckled. "See Cory, antiquing isn't so bad."

They finished paying and exited the store to load everything into Cory's car.

Sebastian leaned against the trunk.

"I'll take one of him too," Melanie whispered. "Let me guess, he's the lawyer?"

Cory nodded as Sebastian straightened and strolled forward. "I saw your car but wasn't sure which building you had disappeared into. Here let me take those."

He took the packages from Melanie while she beamed up at him.

"Hello Sebastian, what a pleasant surprise."

"Hello Adelaide, how are you today?"

"Just fine. We've been shopping as you can see."

His hazel gaze landed on Cory. "Hello Coralea, it doesn't look like you found much, unless some of these are yours?" He lifted the boxes slightly.

"Actually, those are all mine." Melanie interjected with a flutter of her eyelashes.

"This is my friend, Melanie, she's visiting from New Jersey. Melanie, this is Sebastian. He's Aunt Addy's lawyer."

Sebastian only nodded a greeting due to his full hands and smiled at Cory. "I hope I'm a friend too."

"Of course, you are, dear. Why don't we go to the car so Sebastian can put those boxes down?" Her aunt started walking to the car, and they all fell in line with her. Cory opened the trunk for Sebastian to set everything down.

She clenched her fist around the keys in her hand.

He had the same glow or aura she did. Perhaps it was a trick of the sunlight. A result of the abrupt change from interior light to outdoors.

No, in the trunk's shadow it was clear.

Sebastian straightened up and stepped back to close the trunk. Cory couldn't take her gaze from him. Melanie bumped her shoulder, and she glanced over to see her signaling toward him with her eyes. Cory frowned. What?

Melanie rolled her eyes. "Sebastian, would you care to join us for lunch?"

"I'd love to accompany such lovely ladies. Where are you going?"

"I'm going to rest in the car while you young people discuss lunch." Her aunt toddled to the passenger door resting a hand on the car for balance and climbed into the vehicle.

"Me too." Melanie piped in and got in the car.

Sebastian smiled. "You must be pleased your friend is visiting. Is she staying long?"

Cory dragged her gaze to his. What did the aura mean? She had a tough time not stepping forward to examine the shimmering manifestation. She wanted to reach out and try to touch it and see if she felt anything. Was that what caused the power zap the last time they touched?

"Coralea?"

"Hmm...oh, sorry. Melanie is here only until tomorrow, unfortunately."

"So, where would you like to have lunch? The steakhouse we

enjoyed for our dinner date is also open for lunch. If you don't mind a bit of travel, we can head out to the shore, there are some great seafood restaurants to choose from."

"I think it best we stay local. Aunt Addy's tired."

"Of course, then the steakhouse?"

"Yes, that sounds good. We'll meet you there."

Cory kept glancing in his direction as he got in his car and she entered her own. What did it mean? Did he have power too? Was he a witch? Or did they call males warlocks? Sorcerer? Would that make her a sorceress? There appeared to be many differing opinions on that topic, but in Josephine's vision she clearly thought of herself as a witch, so that is what she would stick with.

"What is the verdict, dear?"

Cory glanced at her aunt as she backed out of the parking space. "The steakhouse. Is that okay?"

"Yes, of course. Sebastian will join us?"

She nodded and looked in the rearview mirror. Melanie grinned at her. Cory mouthed the word "What?" Melanie just shook her head and continued to grin.

Only a few moments passed before they arrived at the restaurant. Sebastian opened Aunt Addy's door for her and gave her his arm to escort her into the restaurant.

Melanie whispered to Cory as they walked shoulder to shoulder behind them. "You keep staring at him. You're interested, of course, who wouldn't be? The man is a walking GQ advertisement."

"Shh." The last thing she wanted was for Sebastian to overhear and get the wrong impression. She didn't know how to explain to Melanie why she couldn't stop staring at him though. Maybe she should confess all to Melanie. She needed to confide in someone. Now was not the time, however.

They were escorted to a corner table by the hostess. Sebastian seated Aunt Addy, and Melanie took the chair next to her, leaving Cory to sit between her aunt and Sebastian or Melanie and Sebastian. She sat next to Aunt Addy. Melanie would fill any gaps in the conversation, which would allow Cory to think about the possibilities and consequences of Sebastian sharing the same aura as herself.

She was right. Melanie chatted away with Sebastian and Aunt Addy throughout their meal. Sebastian, however, persistently attempted to include her in the conversation.

"I'm going to visit the ladies' room. Cory, join me?" Melanie stood. Her words were phrased as a question, but her eyes demanded an affirmative answer. Cory stood and followed her friend.

Once they entered, Melanie quickly checked the stalls to confirm they were alone and then faced her with her hands propped on her hips. "Okay, dish. What's going on? Are you interested in him, or not? First you couldn't take your eyes off him, and now you're ignoring his diligent attempts to engage you in conversation."

Cory rubbed her forehead. "I can't explain right now, but I wasn't staring because I'm interested in him. I'm not. I mean, he's a very attractive man, and I was flattered by his attention, but...no."

"Okay, you can't explain now, but later you will fill me in?"

"Yes."

"Fair enough." Melanie looped her arm around Cory's. "So, can I make a play for him then?"

Cory laughed. "Be my guest."

Melanie sighed. "Unfortunately, I think he's pretty focused on you, but maybe once he gets the message it's not going to happen, I can heal his broken heart."

"His heart will not be broken, Mel. We had one date."

"He's awfully persistent after one date, don't you think?"

Cory gazed at Sebastian as they approached the table. "Maybe he has ulterior motives."

Melanie squeezed her arm. "You think he's dangerous to you?"

"I'll explain later, okay?"

Melanie nodded and put a wide smile on her face as she slid into her chair. "So, who's ready for dessert?"

Chapter Fourteen

"Holy shit!"

Melanie and Cory sat cross-legged on Cory's bed facing one another with a plant between them. Cory had just finished explaining all about the puzzle boxes, the vision, and her powers. She had demonstrated her abilities by making the plant grow.

Her best friend stared hard at the plant. "You're not messing with me, are you? A film crew isn't hiding in the closet ready to jump out and say, gotcha or anything?"

"Come on, Mel, you know me better than that."

"Yeah well, never thought you were a witch either." She leaned over and slapped Cory's knee lightly. "Dang girl, you're a witch! How awesomely cool is that!"

Laughing, Cory shook her head. Melanie always made her laugh when she started talking in slang. It was so incongruous with her prim looks.

"You really think Sebastian is a witch too, and might be pursuing you as some sort of couple of centuries year old grudge?"

"I know it sounds insane, but what other explanation is there for the aura? I'm probably grasping at straws here. Even if he has power, it doesn't mean he has anything to do with the ones who were after

Josephine. But he is being persistent, and honestly, I never got the feeling he was all that into me."

"What do you mean?"

"He says the right things, and is incredibly charming and attentive, but I get the impression it's a show. Everything he does seems orchestrated for a purpose."

Melanie scooted down to lie back against the pillows. "Some people are like that, have to plan every decision and step, but I see what you're saying. You think there is no real emotion behind his words or actions?"

"Like that time he kissed me, it was very pleasant, but it also felt rather practiced. You know what I mean?"

Cory got up and put the plant away. Melanie rolled to her side and leaned on her elbow, propping her head up with her hand. "I think you need to avoid him until we figure all this out. There's no reason to take any unnecessary chances. It's obvious you aren't that into him, anyway. He'll get the message."

"And if he doesn't?"

Melanie stood up and hugged her friend. "Then we'll figure that out too. One step at a time. Now, the first step is to do some major research —on the down low, of course. Which just so happens to be my specialty. Melanie Proctor, Librarian extraordinaire, at your service."

Her confidence buoyed Cory's spirits. She didn't feel so alone in this anymore. Confiding in Melanie was the right decision. A fresh pair of eyes, ears, and brain might help her make sense of it all.

Avoiding Sebastian seemed the safest plan, but if he had powers, and if he was pursuing her because he suspected she did too, then what was she going to do? What was his motive? Could he really be connected to what happened to Josephine almost two centuries ago?

If she could see his aura, it stood to reason he could see hers too.

FINN HESITATED a second before opening his front door with a yank. He was a straightforward kind of guy, he said what he meant, and he did what he said he would. He'd said he would stop by before Melanie left today, and that was what he would do. All the mixed signals Cory sent his way had him questioning his every move, and that needed to stop. He didn't have time for that kind of bullshit.

Her words said she wasn't interested in a hook up, but now and then her eyes hinted at something else. She sure hadn't liked her friend flirting with him yesterday, but the question was if it was because she was jealous, or if she was watching out for her friend. That was a bit insulting to both of them though.

He stalked across the yard between their houses and knocked on the back door. His mood wasn't exactly conducive to a visit, but his word was his word.

"Finnegan, what a welcome surprise. Come in, come in." Addy stepped back and walked to the stove. "The girls are in the living room. I was in the process of making some tea. Would you like some, or anything else?"

"No thank you. I just stopped by to say bon voyage to Melanie. I told her I would."

"Oh, that's sweet, dear. You run along to the living room. I'll be in in a minute."

"Anything I can help you with?"

"No, no, it's just a cup of tea." She shooed him away, so he meandered into the living room.

Cory and Melanie had their heads close together on the settee and were whispering about something. Almost immediately, Cory's midnight blue eyes spotted him. She tapped her fingers on Melanie's thigh, and Melanie stopped whispering as her gaze met his. He had caught the word Sebastian, but he had no idea of the context. A deep grin bloomed on Melanie's face, and she rose from the cushions and sashayed her way over to him.

"Finn, I was hoping you'd show up."

He glanced from her to a still seated Cory, who was frowning. He dragged his gaze back to Melanie. "Told you I would. When are you heading out?"

"After lunch. You're a man of your word, are you Finn?"

He shrugged. "Sometimes it's all a guy's got."

She tilted her head to the side and perused his face. "I like you."

He choked on a laugh. "I like you too."

She grinned and grabbed hold of his arm. "Come sit. Tell me something about yourself, Finn. You're a mechanic, aren't you? What led you in that direction?"

Melanie led him to the sofa and directed him to sit in the middle. She sat down so he was sandwiched between her and Cory. Cory's warmth branded his side. He resisted the urge to lean into her. The woman sat rigidly with her arms clenched around her middle.

Finn cocked his head toward Melanie. "I grew up working in my uncle's garage. I had a knack for fixing cars. Worked as a mechanic in the Air Force. After I got out, I attended school for it, and started working on high end sports cars." He shrugged. "One thing led to another. I decided I wanted a change of pace and place. Found a garage for sale and bought it."

"Everyone has a story. It always fascinates me how the circumstances of someone's life shapes their decisions. For instance, if you had never had an uncle with a garage, would you have discovered your talent for cars, or would your life have gone in another direction?"

Finn smiled at her. "Can't really say for sure, though I gravitated to them from as far back as I can remember. And you? What do you do? What circumstances shaped you?"

"Books. Love them. They were my escape growing up and continued into adulthood. I'm a librarian."

"You don't look like any librarian I've ever seen."

Melanie laughed. "I'll choose to take that as a compliment."

"You should."

Addy entered the living room with a cup of tea. "You sound like you're having an enjoyable time. Can I get anyone anything?"

They all answered negatively, and she sat down in the wing-back chair facing the settee. "Girls did you tell Finnegan about your finds yesterday?"

"Finds?"

"We shopped at this marvelous antique store in town. I spent entirely too much money, but I am thrilled anyway. Cory even found a lovely watercolor, didn't you, Cory?"

He glanced at Cory. She gave him a narrow-eyed look. "Yes."

"We ran into Sebastian in town and had a delightful lunch with him." Addy sipped her tea as both Melanie and Cory remained silent.

"Did you? He pops up a lot. When does he work?"

Melanie snorted softly next to him, and he glanced at her to see her frowning down at the floor. Did she not like Sebastian? Was that what the two of them had been discussing when he walked in? Melanie telling Cory to steer clear of the slick talking lawyer? His estimation of her rose by the minute.

"Melanie, I hope you will be able to come back and stay for a longer visit this summer."

"Thank you, Addy. I hope to come back in a few weeks, maybe for a few days instead of only a weekend. We're changing the computer system at work, so it's been hectic lately. It should be finished within in the next week or so though."

"It would be nice if you could take that week off you've been mentioning for what seems like forever. You need a vacation, Mel."

Melanie sighed. "I know, but no one manages the library exactly like I want them too. I may have a tiny control issue."

"May have?"

Melanie leaned forward to stick her tongue out at Cory. Cory laughed and returned the gesture. Finn shifted in his seat. He could supply a few other suggestions for Cory's tongue.

CORY'S EYES FILLED, and she cleared her throat. She stood next to Melanie's loaded car while Melanie started the car and then hopped out to stand in front of her.

"Don't you dare cry. If you do, I'll be bawling the whole way home."

Melanie had already said her goodbyes to Aunt Addy inside the house. Finn had left a little while ago, and Melanie had given him a big hug which he returned.

"I'm going to miss you, Mel."

"Ditto, but I am going to take that vacation, so I'll be back. Hopefully, with a ton of answers for you and your little problem."

"Little problem?" Cory laughed. Melanie always made everything seem so doable.

"Yes, and I expect daily updates. We'll compare notes on what we've discovered."

Melanie wrapped her arms around Cory and rocked back and forth. "Love you."

"Love you too, Mel. Drive safe."

Melanie blew her a kiss and got into her car. She shut the door and rolled down the window. "Cory, I also expect to hear you've jumped that man's bones."

Cory blinked. "What man?"

Melanie smirked at her. "Please, you know dang well, what man. Finn."

Cory swiveled to look behind her at his house. There was no movement that she could see. It didn't look like he was home, but she wasn't taking any chances. She stepped forward to the car. "Hush, what on earth are you talking about? You know I have enough on my plate. Besides, he no longer has an interest in me."

"Uh, huh. I notice you're not denying you have an interest in him. Listen friend, that man's eyes devour you every time you look away. He's definitely still interested, and so are you."

She opened her mouth to deny it, but snapped it closed. She couldn't.

"You never know what surprises life has in store for you. Just take a gander at your life recently. I don't want you to let something or someone slip on by because you're afraid of making a mistake or getting hurt. Life is full of possibilities. We need to be open to them."

Cory glared at her friend. "Pot calling the kettle, Mel."

She laughed. "Yeah, yeah, I know. I'm much better at giving advice than taking it." She put the car in reverse. "Take a chance, Cory."

She waved and stood there until her friend's car disappeared out of sight. She glanced at Finn's house before walking back inside her aunt's.

Chapter Fifteen

The car drove into the garage and after a moment the lights turned on in the house. A war of indecision had plagued Cory all day. She couldn't concentrate on anything else.

Her aunt had long since gone to bed. Cory had tried to sleep. She'd gone through the motions of changing into her nightgown and getting in bed, but sleep had eluded her. She was restless.

She had gotten up after the headlights had shown briefly through the window. His bedroom light came on, and suddenly he was there staring up at her.

Cory tensed for a second. Could he see her? Her light wasn't on. She couldn't make out his expression from this distance. He stood with his hands on his hips.

She swallowed hard when he tugged his shirt over his head and walked out of view.

Pacing the length of her bedroom and back several times, her skin felt on fire despite the blast of frigid air from the air conditioner in the window. She glanced out the window again, and then at her door. Cory made her decision.

Tiptoeing down the stairs to avoid the creaky spots, she eased open the front door. She slowly walked across the front porch to the side facing his house. Gripping the railing she bit her lip. Was she being ridiculous? Was she contemplating making a huge mistake? Adding even more turbulence to her life?

His front door opened, and he stood bathed in light. Shirtless, he leaned against the doorway and folded his arms across his chest. Waiting for her to decide?

The cool, soft grass tickled her toes as she traipsed across the lawn. The full moon guided her steps. She hesitated as she stepped into the pool of light shining from his house. His gaze ensnared hers, and he straightened in the doorway, watching her, but still not saying a word.

The brick step was rough against her feet as she gripped the iron railing and took the first step. His gaze raked her from head to toe.

Finn strode forward and wrapped his arm around her waist. Lifting her over the last couple of steps and into his arms as his mouth captured hers in a devouring kiss.

Cory slid her arms over his shoulders, and behind his neck. Her fingers delved into the thick strands of his hair while her body melted against his.

He backed her into the house, kissing her the entire time. Closing the door, he leaned against it—dragging her pliant body flush to his. Every inch of his hard body plastered the front of her.

Strong hands stroked her flesh, massaging her shoulders and back. Then inching their way around her hips, up her abdomen, and cupping her breasts. Shivers of pleasure danced over her sensitized skin.

Their tongues battled as their hands explored. The heat from his skin warmed her palms as she smoothed them over the hard muscles of his shoulders and back.

Finn palmed the cheeks of her butt and compelled her against him as he switched their positions against the door. She gasped when sandwiched between the cool metal door and the heat of his aroused body. He lifted her thigh and wrapped her leg over his hip for a tighter fit. A tingling, hot pleasure spread up her body. Cory moaned. She wanted more of him.

His hands delved under her baby doll nightgown to her unfettered breasts. He shaped and molded them as his mouth left hers to trail across her cheek and down her neck. His teeth grazed across her skin, and she clutched his shoulders.

Finn nipped gently on her shoulder before lowering his hands and lifting her up. She wrapped her arms and legs around him as he carried her down a short hall to his bedroom.

As he set her down on the bed, his hands grasped the edge of her nightgown sliding it up. She raised her arms to accommodate him. His gaze never left her as he hastily removed his jeans and briefs. She leaned back on her elbows to appreciate the view.

Placing one knee on the bed on the outside of her leg, he traced a hand up the inside of her thigh, while his other hand supported his weight as he lowered himself over her.

Cory stared into Finn's eyes as his hand played with her, wringing gasps of pleasure from her lips. Her eyes slid closed, and her hips surged against his hand as the intensity built.

The wet heat of his mouth encircled her nipple and tugged. He divided his attention between her breasts as bliss raced along her nerve endings. A soft cry erupted from Cory as she melted against the bed.

Finn quickly sheathed himself in a condom before returning to her. Inch by inch he filled her. She raised her knees and opened to him even more.

Her hands surveyed his chest before clenching over his back when he began to thrust. His mouth seized hers in a devastating kiss.

Ecstasy surged inside Cory. She wrenched her mouth from his and gasped against his shoulder as the orgasm exploded inside her.

A harsh groan rasped her ear as he followed her over. Finn held her close as the fervor mellowed.

"I'm going to be really pissed off if this is just a wet dream."

A shocked instant of silence held her motionless before a full-blown laugh escaped from Cory.

Finn chuckled and kissed her shoulder before he got up to dispose of the condom.

Cory scooted up to lean against the pillows while she caught her breath. He was back before the smile died from her face. He leaned over her to kiss her thoroughly. "Guess you're real after all."

Her hand slid down and pinched his butt. "Very real."

"Now you've done it." He started tickling her, which evolved into a wrestling match, and before long they were both much more interested in seeing if the pleasure of the first time was just a fluke.

It wasn't.

Chapter Sixteen

Cool, black potting soil surrounded her fingers. A thin, green and white tendril wrapped around her pinky finger. Cory laughed. The plant behaved like a small child wanting to play or show affection. The roots sought her touch as she transplanted the spider plant to a larger pot.

Memories of the night before with Finn warmed her cheeks. He'd walked her to her door and left her after a scorching kiss. She wasn't sure where this attraction between them was going, but she didn't regret last night. Even if it turned out to be a onetime thing, she was glad for the experience. At least that was what she told herself. *That's my story and I'm sticking to it.*

The chime of an incoming email sounded from her phone. She checked the sender. Melanie. Her friend had thrown herself into exploring the magic world and helping Cory in any way she could. She'd been sending her copies of obscure texts with spells and legends while also trying to trace her ancestor and any information surrounding her.

"Found this one online. Sending you some images. I've also requested some books from other libraries I've come across. We've got this!"

Cory couldn't help but smile. Her friend was the best. She was convinced Melanie could rule the world if she wanted to. Swiping through the images, page after page of various spells and incantations with instructions of when and how to perform them were listed. She shook her head and sighed, the full moon was last night, and it seemed most of these required its presence. Wonder why? This one called for a blue moon, whatever that was.

Hmm. This one was in Latin. Not a required course when she attended school. Rudimentary French was the best she could handle. Wandering out the door to go to the barn and collect some more supplies, she mumbled the words trying to derive their meaning.

A surge of power vibrated her body. She stopped abruptly and whirled around, searching around her.

"Oh my God!"

The apple tree she had just passed which marked the beginning of the orchard was covered in deep red fully ripened apples. In June.

Frantically looking to see if anyone had witnessed the odd event, Cory ran to an empty bucket determined to get rid of the evidence. How could she explain an apple tree ready for harvest a good three months early?

Returning with the bucket she began picking every apple she could grasp. The bucket rapidly overflowed with apples, and she ran to the barn for another bucket.

"Please, please, please." She stretched to her tiptoes snagging the ruby red apples from their branches. One by one the branches bent toward her, and the apples dropped to the ground.

Cory gasped and jumped back. Another shower of apples plunked to the ground in rapid succession.

She looked around wildly before grabbing them all to stuff in the buckets and lugged them to her car trunk.

Luckily, as an employee she always parked in back by the barn leaving the front lot for customers.

Leaning against the wall in the coolness of the barn, she wiped the sweat from her brow. That was the last time she would attempt to read an unknown spell. What had she been thinking? That it was harmless, and likely a load of blarney.

"Cory? Are you all right?"

Cory straightened from the wall and faced Alec, forcing a small smile to her lips. "I'm fine, just resting for a minute. It's hot out there."

He made his way over to her. His kind, weathered face wrinkled in concern. "You're flushed. Are you feeling okay? Perhaps you should go home."

"Oh no, I'm fine, really."

"Well, at least have some water and stay out of the sun. I don't want you overtaxing yourself. It's easy to get dehydrated in the summer heat."

Cory touched his arm and smiled. "I will, Alec. I'm fine, thank you." His gaze followed her as she walked back to the greenhouses.

Note to self, magic is amazingly real.

⊱⊱⊶ ⊷⊰⊰

LIGHTS FLASHED BEHIND HER. A quick glance in her rearview mirror revealed a dark sedan flashing its headlights. What on earth? Cory slowed down and looked again. It was Sebastian.

Her phone rang, and her Bluetooth picked up notifying her of an incoming call. He was calling.

Can't really ignore him when he's right behind me, now can I? She pressed the button to answer, as she searched the road ahead for a public place to stop. There was none.

"Hello?"

"Hello, Coralea. There's a turn off up ahead, take it. We need to talk."

"About what?"

"I'll explain in a moment."

"I'm in a hurry, Sebastian. Can't we talk another time, or over the phone?"

"No, this is best done in person, and time is of the essence."

"Well then, how about you follow me back to Aunt Addy's and we can talk there."

"This is best done in private. There's the turn."

Cory gripped the steering wheel. Indecision warred inside her. If she pulled over, and he meant her harm, she was in the middle of nowhere.

Her magic was unreliable. What if she couldn't defend herself? Was she being crazy? He'd done nothing to suggest he meant her harm. She'd based her worries on a mysterious glow and her admittedly unfounded suspicions.

She turned left at the turnoff. A narrow dirt road meandered before her. Where did this go? She slowed to stop as his car crowded behind her.

Frantically texting Melanie while keeping her gaze peeled on Sebastian as he approached her car, she told her friend what was happening in case he had bad intentions. Cory exited the message application and slid her phone beneath her. She hadn't been able to check what she sent. Hopefully it hadn't autocorrected her to send an illegible message, or something so dire Melanie panicked and called the police, the military, or any other emergency number she could find.

Lowering her window, she forced a tight smile on her lips. "What is so important, Sebastian? I'm running late. People are expecting me." Couldn't hurt to slip that in and let him know she'd be missed.

He stared down at her. He didn't smile. His gaze searched her face, and then he sighed. "Have you been avoiding me, Coralea?"

Absolutely! "No, of course not. I've just been exceedingly busy with my new job and all. Sebastian, I explained to you why I wasn't interested in dating right now." Was that what this was about? Had anyone ever turned him down before?

"What about D'Orsey?"

She tried to prevent the blush she could feel heating her cheeks, but it proved to be a fruitless endeavor. Damn it, what was she supposed to say? They weren't dating, not exactly. They'd had sex. Fantastic sex. She winced. Her face was probably the color of a fire engine.

"It's really such a shame."

Cory glared up at him. All right, she probably could've handled it better, but wasn't he taking it a bit far? "What is?"

"I am sorry, Coralea."

For what? His features grew indistinct as the world around her appeared to tilt. Black spots danced across her vision, and her limbs grew heavy.

Her world went dark.

Chapter Seventeen

Consciousness teased the edges of Cory's mind. Weakness permeated her limbs. A rough material irritated her skin. Her eyelashes fluttered open to reveal a wall of blurry gray in front of her face. An unpleasant mixture of odors assailed her nose. Her mouth was dry as a desert.

"Drink this. It will help."

Cory flipped over, and the world tilted out of focus. Sebastian stood in front of her holding out a bottle of water. Her frantic gaze took in her surroundings. She was in the open trunk of her car. The bastard had knocked her out and put her in the trunk of her own car! She smacked the bottle out of his hands. The motion caused her to sway and fall back against the bottom of the trunk.

"Or not." Sebastian glanced at the water bottle on the ground and then back to her. "You're dehydrated. You need the water." He picked up the bottle and casually handed it to her once again.

Her limbs shook as she attempted to support herself. *Think Cory!* What did he want from her? She needed to stay calm and focused. She needed that water.

Snatching it from his hands, she diligently checked the seal. It appeared intact. Could he have injected it somehow?

"For what it's worth, it's just water. Not that I expect you to believe me."

Cory glared at him before wrenching open the bottle with shaky hands and gulping down the entire contents. He handed her another and she polished it off as well after examining the container.

She felt halfway normal. If sitting in the trunk of her car after being abducted could ever feel normal. "What do you want from me? Why did you do this?"

Cory adjusted her position in the trunk while surreptitiously cataloging her surroundings. They appeared to be at the edge of a small meadow surrounded by trees. His car was parked behind hers on a dirt road. The same dirt road he had her turn into most likely. Which meant she knew where to go if she escaped. She wouldn't have to waste precious moments blindly fleeing through the woods while she figured out where she was.

"To talk."

"Talk? You knocked me out and abducted me to talk? Not an effective way to engage someone in conversation, Sebastian. Did you ever think to ask?"

"I believe I tried on several occasions if you recall. You rebuffed me each time."

He stood with his hands casually resting in the pockets of his trousers, as if they were just having a pleasant chat. He returned her glance with a bland stare. Was he insane? Should she try to reason with him? Placate him? Play along? Act weak and look for an opening to escape?

"All right, obviously you have my attention, and I'm at your mercy. What do you want to talk about?"

Perhaps she should try to sound more like a scared, simpering female in distress and less hostile captive, but she'd like nothing better than to kick him in the balls. The son of a bitch!

She narrowed her eyes as he gave her a one-sided smirk and a tiny dimple appeared. He thought this was amusing?

"Coralea, I find you interesting, and that is saying a great deal, as nothing has interested me for some time."

Well, bully for him. Found her interesting, did he? How interesting would he find her when she knocked him on his ass?

Vines climbed the nearby trees, seeking precious sunlight, circling branches and trunks like giant snakes. Cory delved deep inside for her powers. The answering surge steadied her as she glanced up at him through her lowered lashes. "And what do you find so interesting?" Shifting to her knees she feigned a weakness she no longer felt and grasped the edges of the trunk in readiness.

The vines wrapped around his ankles and yanked him off his feet. She sprang from the trunk and raced to the front of her car, praying the keys were still in the ignition. If not, she had a spare hidden under the wheel well in one of those nifty security boxes, but that would take precious seconds she didn't have.

Wrenching the door open, her gaze frantically searched the ignition. Yes! The keys were there.

The door slammed shut, knocking her on her ass when she leaped back to avoid being hit.

A soft chuckle announced his presence before he loomed over her. "Nicely done, Coralea, but you'll have to do better than that."

She glared up at him. One question had been answered. He had powers. Was that how he had knocked her out without touching her? Nifty trick. She wished she knew how to do that.

The tall grass tickled her bare skin. The blades fluttered against her in a soothing pattern. Could she somehow lure him to the trees and knock him out with a branch, or even skewer him? She felt quite murderous.

The energy flowed into her from the plants, burgeoning her powers. Small twigs and branches flew through the air pelting Sebastian. He threw up his arms to protect himself as she scrambled to her feet. Since Sebastian was between her and her car, she twisted to run in the opposite direction toward his vehicle and the road.

The slap of power knocked her to her knees and left her gasping for air. Sweat poured from her as weakness spread. She fought it, but it left her floundering. She braced herself on her hands and knees as his feet appeared in her line of vision.

"Your follow through needs work."

Cory scowled. Tilting her head, she watched as he gingerly plucked a twig from his hair and smoothed the strands back in place.

"This can go one of two ways. One, we continue to fight and you lose. I deliver you to your own personal hell as I have been ordered to do. Or second, you listen and learn."

Sebastian raised one imperious eyebrow. "The choice is entirely yours. I don't care either way."

She leaned back on her heels, resting her hands on her thighs while she stared at the ground mulling over his words. He was more powerful than her. He'd made that abundantly clear. Someone had ordered him to abduct her. The question was who and why? Most importantly, did he mean Hell literally?

"I believe I'll take option two."

"Sound choice."

He held out his hand. She eyed it like a coiled rattlesnake. Was he serious? Although a bit unsteady, she stood without help.

She ambled to her car and leaned against it for support. Folding her arms across her middle, she stared at him, waiting.

"I'm going to get you some water from my car. If you attempt another escape, option two is off the table. Understood?"

Her mouth was again dry as parchment, so she nodded slowly. She had no intention of doing anything until she had some answers, and she was in no hurry to be delivered to the hell he mentioned.

Handing her a bottle as he returned, he opened his own and drank. Cory did the same. Drinking deeply at first and then taking a few smaller sips. "I'm listening."

Sebastian capped his empty bottle before taking hers and tossing them both in the back of his car. He walked back to her and surveyed her from head to toe.

"Is the weakness gone?"

"Yes, pretty much. Are you going to tell me how you did that? Better yet, teach me? You said listen and learn."

His single dimple appeared briefly. "You can't be taught that trick."

"Try me."

He sighed. "You really are clueless, aren't you?"

Cory straightened against the car. "I beg your pardon?"

"Power is derived from the four elements: fire, air, water, and earth. You can only have power from one element. Nature's way of checks and balances. Yours is from the earth, obviously. Control of plants, more specifically."

"Where does your power come from?"

"What do you think?"

Well, he can knock her out without a touch. He slammed the car door without touching it. "Air?"

"No."

"Then how did you slam the door, or knock me out without touching me?"

"The door was simply a shove of power. You can learn that given enough time and practice. What is the human body mostly composed of?"

Cory shrugged. "Skin? I'm not a doctor." Although her mother was. What would her mother think of all this? A laugh threatened to bubble up her throat. Perhaps she was becoming hysterical, because she couldn't help but be amused by the thought of her mother's reaction.

"The human body is more than half water. Each individual is slightly different of course, some have more than others."

"So water is your element?"

Sebastian nodded once. "What you experienced is rapid dehydration. A little will weaken, a lot can render the person unconscious."

Didn't seem particularly fair. How could she fight against someone who could simply knock her out every time? Water appeared to be the more powerful element at the moment.

"I can teach you to resist it, up to a point."

That was interesting. He would teach her how to fight his magic? "Why? Why would you teach me how to resist your powers?"

"Because you're strong, not just with power, but strength of will. I believe you can learn to fight. With the right instruction, you could help alter the course of both our lives."

"And why would I want to do that?"

"Remember option one? It leads to a continued life of servitude for me, and most likely death for you, or at the very least you'd wish for death."

Chapter Eighteen

That didn't sound promising in the least. Death, or wishing for it, was something she wanted to avoid. Life of servitude? What did that mean?

"Who exactly do you serve and why? And what does it have to do with me?"

Sebastian stood at ease with his hands once more in his pockets staring off into the distance. His gaze rested on Cory for a moment before he finally replied. "It all centers around power. You have it, others want what you have. If they can't control the power through you, then they'll take it from you."

"Take it from me how? People can do that? And what do you mean control me?"

"He's not what I would describe as a person, not anymore anyway. His humanity, if he ever had any, has long since disappeared. He's the only one I know of who can steal another's power."

"Who is he, and how does he steal powers?"

"The exact process is known only to him, but it is a ritual which can only be done during a total solar eclipse. The next one is less than two months away, August twenty-first. Which is why we don't have much time. You need to learn to access your power and control it at will, or you won't have a chance."

Cory rubbed the goosebumps spreading up her arms. A few months ago, her life was hard enough, her marriage had ended badly, she had no job or home, but at least she had her health. Now, it looked like someone wanted to take that from her as well.

"Stealing my power will kill me?"

His gaze delved into hers. "Most likely. There have been a few to survive it over the years, but not for long, and it was not an existence I would wish on anyone."

Okay, not a viable option, got it. "What did you mean about controlling me and my power?"

Sebastian sighed. "Unfortunately, or fortunately, depending on how you look at it. That is not likely to be an option for you. He's desperate for power and you're the only outsider with power right now." He shrugged. "Of course, if he decided your power was more valuable to him than another's then he wouldn't hesitate to take theirs instead if he thought he could control you. I have my doubts whether you could manage the subservient role, however."

Cory's foot tapped. "Are you saying if I could convince him I would join his little band of witches, or warlocks, or whatever you call yourselves then he might keep me around instead of killing me and taking my power? Yet, at the expense of one of your members?"

Could she convince someone that she would serve them to save herself? Depends on what she had to do. Could she do it, knowing someone else would die in her place? Well, hell, were they evil? That might help.

"Witches and essentially yes."

Cory paced the length of her car and back. A band of witches were out to steal her power, most likely killing her in the process, or making her wish she was dead. There was a slight chance she could convince them she wanted to join them instead, but then someone else would die in her place. Someone who apparently was okay with her dying though, right?

"What did you mean by serving? What precisely does that entail?"

"Performing magic rituals, seeking and bringing witches to him, and in your case getting pregnant by him and bearing a little witch to inherit your power which he can raise and control."

Bile rose in her throat. Stopping to glare at him, Cory clenched her fists. "Excuse me?"

A tiny dimple appeared at the corner of his mouth. "Look Coralea, I told you, you wouldn't like the options. You are a full-grown woman. He will only see two purposes for you. Take your power or use you to bear a child who will inherit your power whom he can control. Killing you after you do, of course."

Nausea churned in her stomach. Bear a child with an evil madman so it could be raised to do more evil? Not going to happen. That left only one option, learn to fight in a little less than two months' time. Was it even possible? What choice did she have? If Sebastian was to be believed, none.

"Is it possible to teach me in such a short time?"

"There is no other option for you, so it better be possible. You have to learn."

"Who will I have to fight, and what will it accomplish? Won't it just be a delay, or is that the point? Delaying until the next solar eclipse? Allowing me to get stronger?"

"No, the goal is to kill him once and for all. He's weakened right now. Which is why he needs your power so badly. It may be our only opportunity. He hasn't fed since the total eclipse in Russia in 2008, and the one he took wasn't strong."

Cory recoiled. "Fed?"

"I told you. He needs the powers he steals during the total solar eclipse to survive."

"Like a power vampire?"

"Yes, he's over three centuries old."

She opened her mouth and then shut it. She looked down at her arms and reached over to pinch herself hard on the bicep.

"What are you doing?"

She clenched her teeth and pinched harder. "This is a nightmare, and I want to wake up."

Sebastian sighed. "Welcome to my world. The only way to wake up and free yourself is learning to fight, like I've told you repeatedly. Now stop behaving like a child and let's get started. I can always go back to the original plan and deliver you to him. Don't make me regret giving you a chance."

Cory glared at him through narrowed eyes. "Don't make it sound like your motives are altruistic. You want my help to end your life of servitude, as you put it."

"Just so, but I will save my own hide first. So, if you don't step up to the plate and stop dithering, I have a backup plan."

"Duly noted, I can't trust you. Thanks for the warning."

"You can trust me to train you, as long as you put in the effort and focus required."

"How many witches are in your little group, and how many will I have to fight? Will you be one of them?"

"It's called a coven. He's been building one he has complete control over. He can't wield each power himself, so he makes sure he controls those who do. A full coven is made up of twelve, three from each element of power. He was in a rage once and let it slip that he destroyed his original coven. I don't know all the details. I know he's been hunting the descendants of that original coven. You, being the latest. There are currently five members, including him and myself. He has a tendency to lose his temper and kill members who don't perform exactly how he dictates. Others he sacrificed over the years to sustain himself."

A shudder rippled through her. "You didn't answer how many I would have to fight or whether you would be one of them."

"It depends. If I'm able to sway others to our side, then there will be less."

Cory closed her eyes briefly. He wasn't answering her question completely, but then maybe his avoidance was the answer. He'd already told her he would save himself first. She would learn from him, but never trust him. He could betray her at any moment. She had experienced betrayal. She hoped she had learned from her mistakes. She would be ready and prepared. What else could she do?

"Why do you serve him, and who is he? The more knowledge I have the more I will be prepared."

An uneasy silence stretched between them. She started to think he wouldn't answer her.

"He threatens someone I've sworn to protect. Who he is, is the same one who pursued your ancestor across the ocean after destroying their coven. He's been searching for your line and power for centuries. He's my father."

Chapter Nineteen

"We can get fake passports and disappear. I have savings, always wanted to travel, but never got around to it. You leave now, and I'll have everything ready by the time you get here."

Tears welled in her eyes, and she took a deep breath. "Mel, you're the best friend ever, but running isn't the answer. If Sebastian is to be believed, and about this I do, then they would find me. Now that my powers have been unlocked, and until I learn how to control it, I'm like a beacon to those with power. I'd be delaying the inevitable and putting your life in danger. Not going to happen. In fact, I probably shouldn't talk to you about any of this anymore and you definitely need to stop researching it. They could track you somehow."

"Bullshit."

Cory sat down on her bed and leaned back against the pillows, closing her eyes. What the hell was she going to do?

"I'm not an idiot, Cory. No one is tracking the research I'm doing. I know how to cover my tracks. Being a paranoid, conspiracy theory junkie comes in handy in this type of situation. You try to cut me out and I'm going to move in with you. I'll be stuck to you like super glue. I appreciate the consideration for my safety, but there's no way in hell I'm letting you travel this road alone. Got it?"

Cory snorted. She'd do it too. Staring at the ceiling, she tried to think what the right thing to do was.

"I mean it, Cory."

"I know you do, but I couldn't handle it if something happened to you because of me."

"How do you think I'd feel if something happened to you and I did nothing to prevent it? I need to try to help you. It's what people who care about each other do. Besides, two heads are better than one. Now, the discussion is over. You're not persuading me to back off. We need to focus on getting you strong and ready for this battle. I'm going to find out all I can about Sebastian and his demonic family, and you're going to learn from him while staying on your guard at all times. Don't trust him, Cory."

"Witches, not demons."

"Yeah well, witchy family doesn't sound evil enough."

Cory chuckled. "I love you, Mel. Thank you."

"Love you too. Promise me you won't keep anything from me. I don't want to worry about any secrets."

She battled with herself over the decision. Selfishly, she wanted to share this nightmare with someone she trusted. Wanted to be able to talk to someone and not feel like she was alone, or insane. But she truly could never forgive herself if something happened to Melanie because of her. She should've lied when Melanie called her frantic over the text messages she had received. Instead, the truth about Sebastian and his so-called mission and proposal had tumbled from her lips in an avalanche of disbelief and terror. Now, her best friend was dragged even deeper into this mess with her.

"Cory?"

"Of course." She had to protect her. In a few days, she would come up with a believable story why it was all resolved and there was nothing more to worry about.

"The words, Cory, I want the words, and I'll know if you're lying. You suck at it."

"Damn it, Mel." Cory rolled her eyes. She did suck at it. Another reason she could never pretend to go along with Sebastian's family, they'd be on to her in a heartbeat the first time she had to lie.

"Still waiting."

"I promise, okay?" She would have to figure out a way to keep Melanie safe while keeping her in the loop.

"Good. Worrying about secrets between us would just take crucial energy and time away from what we need to be focused on. I don't want to second guess what you aren't telling me and then have to manipulate you into telling me."

"So, you admit you're a manipulator?"

"Please, like that was ever a secret."

Cory swung her legs off the bed and stood up. "Your turn to promise. Promise me you will take every precaution and no chances. I don't want you endangered by my mess."

"Easy promise to make. There's no need for you to spend an instant worrying about that. I am always super careful, and now I'll make sure to be doubly so, okay?"

"Okay."

"So, no more secrets, right?"

"I already promised, Mel." She bit her lip. "Although, there is one thing I haven't told you."

"Spill."

"I had sex with Finn."

THE CHILLY AIR from the fridge provided a short reprieve from the sweltering summer temperature. Aunt Addy's house had never been updated with central air conditioning. There were window units in the bedrooms, but the common areas grew uncomfortable on days like today. Her heated skin was sticky from the humidity despite the shower she had just taken.

Cory had dressed in shorts and a tank top, anticipating working outside in her aunt's gardens to help gather her thoughts and come up with a solid plan to deal with the surreal life she found herself in, but it was just too hot and humid.

The knock at the back door made her jump and jarred her from her musings. Shutting the refrigerator, she pivoted on her toes and stared at the windowpanes of the door. Trepidation caused her to hesitate, but logic dictated what threatened her wasn't likely to come calling at her aunt's back door. That and the fact she could see Finn's familiar form.

What on earth was she going to say to him? She hadn't seen or spoken to him since Sunday night, or technically Monday morning. She hadn't had a chance to really think about their next meeting.

Deciding to open the door and find out what he wanted instead of trying to guess, she marched to the door and swung it open, pasting a smile on her face. He probably wanted to speak to her aunt about something, anyway.

"I was beginning to think you weren't going to open the door."

Of course, if she could see him through the door, he could see her too. The light from the fridge probably made it even easier.

"Thought never crossed my mind." Wonder why? It should have. She should avoid him and any other distraction like the plague. She was in a literal life and death situation. Getting any further involved with Finn had to be a terminally bad idea. She needed to put on the brakes. "I was simply lost in thought for a moment." She stepped back. "Come in. It's not much cooler inside, but I'd like to keep as much of the hot air out as possible."

Finn sauntered past her and leaned against the counter with his arms folded across his chest and ankles crossed. She couldn't help but smile. Even in this heat he wore jeans.

"Where's Addy?"

She was right, he was here for her aunt after all. Her shoulders deflated a bit. Probably for the best, she had enough on her plate. "Aunt Addy won't be home until late this afternoon. Do you want me to pass on a message?"

His leisurely gaze traveled over her. A tingle of awareness danced down her spine. She swallowed and crossed her arms. She needed to keep a distance between them. The other night was a one-time thing.

"No, I'm not here for her."

Oh. Butterflies took flight in her stomach.

"I spoke to Addy yesterday, and she mentioned you had the day off

136

today. Thought you might like to take a ride with me. I have to stop by a friend's house and take a look at his car. His wife is a gardener. She has quite the spread. I thought you might enjoy seeing it."

She should say no. End whatever was between them now before it progressed any farther.

"I have air conditioning in the car."

A laugh burst from her, and she smiled and shook her head. She really shouldn't, but she wanted to. Was it so wrong to want a few hours of reprieve from the crisis looming over her life?

"Did I mention, Sally, his wife, is a great cook and invited us to lunch?"

Cory met his gaze, a negative answer on the tip of her tongue. It melted away. "Give me a few minutes to change."

She turned to go, but he snagged her hand before she took two steps.

"Nope, no point in changing. It's totally casual, and it'll be hot outside looking at her gardens. You'll want to be comfortable. Let's go."

The warmth from his hand encased hers. He didn't seem to be in a hurry to let it go. She shrugged slightly. "Okay but let me grab my purse upstairs."

"Don't need it." He snagged her phone off the table. "Here, that's all you need." He tugged on her hand and she followed him out the door, locking it behind her. She prayed she wasn't making a mistake.

Chapter Twenty

The ivory length of her legs made his palms itch to caress them. Her white shorts and navy-blue tank top hugged her luscious curves. Finn divided his attention between the road and Cory sitting silently in the seat next to him staring out the window. Something was up. The tension radiating from her was like a neon sign since she opened the back door to the house. At first, he thought she intended to brush him off, and pretend the other night had never happened or that it was a mistake and not to be repeated. Which is why he rushed her out of the house before she could think about it too much and change her mind.

He took the entrance ramp to the interstate and glanced at her again. She was lost in her own little world. Hadn't asked any details about their destination. If he went the direct route and asked her straight out what was going on, she'd likely clam up and withdraw further. Cory Bishop was like a finely tuned Ferrari, beautiful on the outside with intricate mechanics underneath the hood. That was okay, temperamental, complicated, sports cars were his specialty.

"I signed up for dog obedience training classes. Bat and I start next week."

"Oh, they're going to train you too? What an excellent idea."

"Very funny, princess, but I suppose it's true in a way. They only work with both the owner and the dog. I thought I would just send Bat and they would train him, but apparently it doesn't work that way."

"What mischief has Bat been getting into now?"

Finn snorted. "Let's see, he's single handedly destroyed two dog beds, and has a personal vendetta against pillows."

Cory's smile stretched wide as she chuckled. "He's quite the handful, isn't he? He's so adorable though, you can't help but forgive him."

"Yeah, he's got that going for him at least."

"Tell me more about your friends we're going to see."

"I met Sam in the Air Force. He was a career officer, while I only served a brief stint, but we hit it off and kept in touch. He's retired now. His wife Sally is a retired school teacher."

"Was he your commanding officer?"

"Yeah, he's the reason I stayed as long as I did. Helped me to see it wasn't for me though. Convinced me to follow my passion for cars."

Cory rested her head against the seat as she studied Finn's handsome profile. He never talked about his family. He'd mentioned learning about cars from his uncle, but that was the extent.

"What about your family? Do they live nearby?" He glanced at her briefly. "No, it's just me. My dad died when I was a kid. My mom passed while I was in the service."

"What about your uncle? The one you worked in the garage for?"

"Uncle Benny, my mom's brother, we went to live with him after my dad died. He passed away before I joined the service."

"I'm sorry, Finn. That must have been a challenging time for you. Losing your family like that. My mother can drive me crazy, but I can't imagine losing her or my dad."

"After my dad died, my mom never got over it. She sort of faded a little bit at a time. She never smiled anymore; nothing brought her any joy. Certainly not her scrawny kid who was always getting into one scrape after another. After another school suspension, she packed up all our stuff and moved us in with Uncle Benny. He was a widower too, no kids. He was strict, but fair. Told me I was going to earn my keep, and I did."

Finn shrugged. "Kept me too busy to get into trouble. Besides, I discovered cars then, and they held more interest than anything else."

He glanced at her and smiled. "Well, except for girls. I got real interested in them too."

Cory chuckled and turned to look out the windshield. "I bet."

FINN EXITED the highway and drove through a large town with shopping plazas and busy streets. The area reminded her a bit of New Jersey. Strange, she no longer thought of it as home. Connecticut was home. She didn't miss the hustle and bustle, or the convenience of the multitude of stores within a five-minute drive. Who would have imagined quiet country living was what she craved?

"This is their place up ahead."

A gray Cape Cod style house with a covered front porch stood at the end of the cul-de-sac. Cory leaned forward and gasped. Gardens stretched from the front of the house and down the sides. Stonewalls edged the property with flowers blooming along the base of them.

"I knew you'd like it."

He drove into the driveway and followed it to the back of the house, where a large barn like garage stood. Raised beds of vegetables grew in rows behind the house.

A wide grin spread across her face. "I love it."

An older man with salt and pepper close-cropped hair stepped out of the garage, wiping his hands on a rag. Finn parked and got out of the car. "What have you done to my baby, Sam?"

Sam laughed and stepped forward to slap Finn on the shoulder. "Good to see you, son. Bout time you decided to visit."

Cory approached slowly, giving the two men a minute to greet one another in privacy. Finn held out his hand to her and smiled. "This is Cory. Cory, this is Sam Barnes. He fancies himself a mechanic."

Sam grinned and grasped Cory's hand. "It's an absolute pleasure to meet you, Cory."

"You too."

Finn suddenly disappeared, and Cory swung around to see him pick up a petite woman with dark hair streaked with silver and spin her around. A startled shriek escaped the woman. "Finnegan D'Orsey, you put me down this instant. You're going to give me a heart attack."

Sam laughed. The woman smacked Finn on the arm, and he put her down with a laugh. She then hugged him close and lightly smacked him again. "Where are your manners? Introduce me to your lovely woman."

Finn took her arm and escorted her over to Cory. "Cory, this is Sally."

Sally grasped Cory's hand with both of hers. "When Finn said he was bringing you to meet us, I was so happy I danced a jig around the kitchen. He's never introduced us to a woman he was dating before."

Cory peeked at Finn waiting for him to correct Sally's interpretation, but he ignored the description and addressed Sam.

"Show me what you've done to her."

Finn looked at Cory. "Sam owns a '69 ZL1 Camaro."

"Oh, that's nice."

Sally laughed and looped her arm around Cory's. "Come dear. While the boys go make goo-goo eyes at an overpriced piece of machinery, you and I can have some iced tea and get to know one another."

"All right, Sally, I'd really love to look at your gardens. I was admiring them as we arrived. They're wonderful."

"Oh, thank you. We can go make goo-goo eyes at my gardens then."

A few hours later they were all sitting in the sunroom after having a delicious and filling lunch. Finn twined their fingers together as he listened to Sam and Sally reminiscing about the time Sam and Finn had found the Camaro at an auction. Sam had purchased it and Finn had helped him refurbish it.

Cory relaxed back against the couch cushion. Her mind drifted, and their voices faded as the sleepless night of the night before caught up with her.

FINN SMILED at his friends and glanced over to where Cory's head rested on the couch. Her eyes drifted shut, and her head slipped down to rest on Finn's shoulder. The tension radiating from her this morning was gone. As the day had progressed, she had relaxed and smiled often, as he had hoped.

He glanced over at Sam and Sally. They watched him with smiles on their faces.

The conclusions they were drawing were clearly etched in their expressions. They saw them as a couple. Sally was probably already planning to include Cory for the holidays. It didn't surprise him. What surprised him was, he didn't seem to mind at all.

Chapter Twenty-One

"Again."

Cory's body ached, her mind was mush, but she took a deep breath and gathered her power. It built like a ball of energy in her core. She sent it blasting outward toward Sebastian who stood about twenty feet away.

With a wave of his hand, he deflected it easily and sent a shot back at her.

Throwing up her hands she tried to deflect it, but it barreled past her attempt and slammed into her, knocking her to the ground.

She lay there, gasping for breath. "Again."

Screw You!

The words screamed in her mind, but she didn't have the breath or the energy to utter them out loud.

Swift steps approached. She slanted open her eyes. Sebastian loomed over her. Not a single blond hair was out of place. His polo shirt and pants weren't skewed in the least. Damn him. He looked like he was out for a casual stroll, rather than having taken part in a magic battle for the past few hours.

Meanwhile, her shorts and shirt were irrevocably grass and dirt stained. She was sure bruises were forming all over her body. She felt like she had gone head-to-head with a heavyweight boxer and lost.

"If it's your intention to blast me into unconsciousness, you're just about there."

"My intention, Coralea, is to prepare you for the coming battle. This is nothing compared to what you will face. Now either get up and try again, or give up, and I'll escort you to my father. Your choice."

He sauntered away. She clenched her fists into the grass beneath her and squeezed her eyes shut. She was sick and tired of him threatening her with that option.

A thump and a curse shot her eyes open.

Sebastian lay face down on the ground. Blades of grass wrapped around his ankles. More shot up over his arms and legs trying to keep him down.

He yanked his arms free and tore the shackles of grass from his ankles.

Cory scrambled to stand and prepared for his retaliation.

He slowly stood and glanced at her as he brushed the remaining blades of grass from his body. "Better, but you need to follow through. Don't stand there waiting for a response. If you manage to get your opponent down, keep them down."

Yeah, I would if I had any idea how I did that in the first place.

"WHAT THE FUCK?" Finn watched Cory exit Sebastian's Mercedes. She stiffly walked up the stairs and into the house without a backward glance. He supposed he should be thankful she didn't give the wanker a kiss goodnight. The urge to walk over and punch him in the face rose inside him, but he was already backing out of the driveway.

A tug on the leash diverted his attention away from the disappearing taillights. Bat had rolled over on his back, wrapping the leash around himself and was busy chewing on it. Finn squatted down and extricated the puppy, rubbing his belly in the process.

"Silly pup."

He scooped up the puppy and headed into the house. He set Bat down on the floor and watched him attack one of his chew toys for a moment. He'd guessed Sebastian was more her type from the beginning. He shouldn't be surprised to be proven right.

A swipe of his hand knocked the plastic thermos from the counter and sent it flying across the kitchen bouncing off the wall and onto the floor.

Bat barreled out of the room disappearing around the corner and down the hallway.

Finn rubbed both his hands over his face, and then stooped to pick up the thermos and put it in the sink. He rested his hands on the edge of the sink and hung his head.

Why the hell was he so pissed off?

It's not like they had any promises between them. They were both free to see other people. In fact, that blonde little number from the diner had been after him for a while. She'd written her number on his receipt the other day and told him to give her a call.

He walked down the hall to his bedroom to look through the receipts he'd tossed on his dresser when he emptied his jean pockets. The small stack of crumbled papers was interspersed with loose change. After finding the receipt in the pile, he yanked out his cell to dial the number.

Tossing his cell phone on the dresser, he walked over to the window and stared up at Cory's window. His interest didn't lie with the blonde, or anyone else but a certain blue-eyed siren.

He dropped on his bed and folded his arms beneath his head, staring up at the ceiling. What the hell was he going to do about it?

Things had been progressing nicely, maybe a tad slower than he'd like. He really wanted to get her back in his bed. One spectacular night was not enough to cure this craving he had for her.

This was bullshit!

Finn stood up and stalked down the hall and out his front door. Bat barreled around the corner as he was shutting the door, so he bent and scooped him up into his arms.

Leaving him home and unattended was never a good idea. He jogged up the front steps and onto the porch of Addy's house. Bat started squirming as Finn knocked on the door.

He glanced down at the wriggling, black ball of fur. "Sorry buddy, but we left your leash at home, and you've proven you can't be trusted." The puppy stopped moving and guilelessly stared up at him.

The door opened, and both Finn and Bat turned to look.

Cory stood in the doorway with a soft smile on her face. She'd obviously just come from the shower. Her wet hair was fashioned into a braid, her face scrubbed clean.

"We need to talk, princess."

Chapter Twenty-Two

Cory focused on Bat, petting and cooing at him, giving herself a moment to think about Finn's words. They sounded a bit ominous. She couldn't handle any more doom and gloom today. She needed a little positivity.

"What about?"

Finn peered past her into the house. "Where's Addy?"

Cory frowned. "Uh, she's playing bridge at a friends' house. Why?" Was something wrong with her aunt?

"Good, that means you're free for dinner. Come on." Finn grabbed her hand and started tugging her out the door.

She dug in her heels and yanked back after stepping down to the porch. "Finn, wait."

Finn looked at her over his shoulder. "What's the problem, princess?"

"Well for one, I don't have any shoes on."

"Here, hold Bat." He dumped the puppy into her arms, and she had no choice but to wrap both arms around him as he started squirming all about and licking her cheek. The click of the front door sounded behind her as Finn closed it.

The world tilted as Finn lifted her into his arms. "Finn! Put me down! What are you doing?"

"You were worried about no shoes, problem solved." He stalked down the stairs and started across the lawn.

"This is ridiculous. I could've simply gotten my shoes. And, what makes you think I want to have dinner with you? You didn't even ask. I could have plans."

He carried her up his front steps and set her down to open the door. He gazed back at her. "Will you have dinner with me, princess?"

Cory sighed and resisted the urge to stamp her foot. She had planned to have a quiet night going over the research Mel had sent her and her own notes while wallowing in self-pity over today's failure in training with Sebastian.

She glanced back at her aunt's house and then at Finn staring at her, waiting for her decision. Bat yipped, and she looked down at him in her arms. His little black body wiggled in delight, and he stared back at her as if he too were waiting for her decision.

Marching past Finn into the house, she mumbled, "You better be able to cook."

"I can cook well enough."

His presence loomed behind her as she walked into his living room. Although she'd been here once before, she hadn't paid attention to any details beyond the general layout of the house that night.

Bat squirmed to get down, and she lowered him to the floor while scanning her surroundings. Black leather sectional, huge flat screen television, recliner, magazines on the coffee table, along with an empty beer bottle. A bachelor's pad to be sure.

The hallway to the right led to his bedroom she recalled, and she had vague impressions of a couple other doorways. An archway opened off the living room. She wandered over to it and peeked into the kitchen. Oak cabinets, stainless steel appliances, and granite countertops. It looked like it had been renovated recently.

"Inspection meet your standards, princess?"

He stood a few feet away with his hands on his hips. Bat played at his feet.

"My only real requirement, if you're going to cook me a meal in it, is that it's clean. But I do like your cabinets. Did you redo the kitchen when you purchased the house, or was it already done?"

Finn walked past her into the kitchen and opened the refrigerator. "I redid it when I bought the place. I don't think anything had been touched since it was built in the sixties. Renovated the bathrooms too. Refinished the floors, added central air, and I had to have the wiring updated."

Chilly air drifted from the ceiling vent above her. "I highly approve of the air conditioning."

He gave her a half smile while he set a couple of steaks on the counter. "Want something to drink?"

"Actually, I'd love one of those beers, if you have another?" Her chin jerked in the direction of the empty bottle in the living room.

Finn grabbed a couple of bottles from the fridge and opened one before handing it to her.

"Thanks."

"We're having steak and potatoes."

"Okay, anything I can do to help?"

"Naw. I'm going to throw them all on the grill. Feel free to check out the rest of the house, or take a seat, whichever you want."

She watched him seasoning the meat for a moment as she took a sip of the ice-cold beer. At first, when he had said they needed to talk she had expected unpleasantness. But then when he had invited or rather demanded she come to dinner, she thought dinner was what he had meant. Watching his stiff back as he wrapped the potatoes in aluminum foil, however, she began to think the talk was still to come.

Turning around, she walked down the short hallway and peeked in the open doorways. First on the right, was a standard three-piece bathroom with white fixtures and black and white floor tile. Next was the spare bedroom, sparsely decorated with a full-size bed, a dresser, and a desk overflowing with papers and a computer. The primary bedroom took up the left side of the house. She stepped into the room. An open door on the left led to a primary bathroom with a large marble tiled walk-in shower.

"It used to be a three-bedroom house with just one bathroom. I combined the two bedrooms on this side into the primary suite."

She glanced around at the sound of his voice to find him leaning against the door jamb.

"Dinner will be awhile. Steaks won't take long once I put them on the grill, but the potatoes need more time."

"Okay. You did a really impressive job with the house."

His gaze remained on her as he took a drink from his bottle of beer. She watched his dark throat move as he swallowed and followed the tan skin down the V-neck of his black shirt with her gaze.

He set the bottle down on his dresser and sauntered over to her. Taking the bottle from her hand, he set that one down as well, before cupping her face in his hands and staring into her eyes.

"Do you know how beautiful you are?"

Cory swallowed and blinked back the sudden wetness in her eyes. She placed her hands on his chest and stretched up on her toes to reach his full lips.

As soon as their lips met, Finn dropped his hands from her face and grasped her waist dragging her body toward him. His tongue sought entrance, and she opened to him. The desire between them exploded.

The silkiness of his black hair caressed her fingers as she slid her hands up to delve into the strands at the back of his neck.

His warm hands slipped beneath her top to explore and massage her back.

Heat and need spread through her body.

Clasping the back of his head, she arched her body into the hard planes of his. Finn's hands slid down to squeeze the cheeks of her ass and fit her against him.

Cory gasped as his mouth left hers to make a hot trail down her neck.

His hands skimmed along her abdomen and grasped her shirt raising it up and over her head. His mouth instantly returned to explore the exposed skin.

The clasp on her bra gave way as he unhooked it and tugged the straps down her arms to dispose of the garment in his way.

He wasted no time. His hands shaped and lifted her breast to the eager warmth of his mouth.

Cory clutched his head to her, as her eyes closed in bliss.

His hands dropped away briefly before sliding beneath her knees and shoulders to pick her up and carry her to the bed. He captured her mouth once again as he lowered her to the cool, soft sheets of the unmade bed.

Goosebumps rose on her flesh when he trailed the backs of his fingers down her torso. Then Finn unbuttoned her shorts and slowly lowered them and her panties down her legs. His mouth followed the path down and back up the opposite leg.

Cory sat up and grabbed hold of his shirt, yanking it up his back. He sat up to take it off, and then stood and removed the remainder of his clothing.

Her gaze trailed from top to bottom, admiring his entire length.

He grabbed a condom from his nightstand drawer and tossed it on the bed before lying on his side next to her. Finn kissed her deeply while letting his hands incite pleasure along all her nerve endings.

Her hands roamed over his back and down to trail along his hardness. His pleasure-filled groan encouraged her, as she stroked and cupped him, learning what pleased him.

"Slow down, princess, or this will be over before it begins." He held her hand still between them as he panted softly.

"Can't," Cory whispered back as she captured his mouth with hers.

A short pleasure-filled groan escaped him when his fingers discovered just how ready she was.

She panted against his shoulder as he delved deep before ripping open the package and donning the condom. Opening for him as he rose above her, she stared up into his eyes.

He entered her slowly, completely. His gaze never left hers. Cory's eyes slid closed in surrender, and her head arched back into the bed.

Finn lowered over her, and his movements increased in depth and speed. His lips burned a path across her shoulder and up her neck before possessing her lips in a drugging kiss.

A hot ball of pleasure burst inside her, radiating out from her core. Her body clenched in ecstasy. Finding his release, Finn clutched her against him.

Their racing hearts beat in rhythm. Sweat dampened skin cooled while they lay in silence in each other's arms.

Finn slowly rose and gave her a soft, deep kiss. "How hungry are you?"

Cory slowly blinked.

"For food."

"Oh, well." Her stomach chose that moment to let out a protesting growl.

Finn chuckled. "I guess I have my answer. I better go check the potatoes and put on the steaks." He gave her another quick kiss before standing up and disappearing into the bathroom.

Cory's limbs refused to function. She remained still, blinking up at the ceiling.

"I know I promised to feed you, but do you have any idea how badly I want to crawl back into bed with you?" Finn stood at the end of the bed staring down at her. He had dragged on his jeans, leaving them unbuttoned and clearly showing the truth of his words.

She smiled. "There's always after dinner."

Chapter Twenty-Three

A refreshing breeze whispered through the leaves of the trees—cooling the back of her neck. The sun lowered on the horizon, and shades of peach, pink, and yellow stretched across the sky. The scent of grilled food still spiced the air. Cory sank back against the cushioned chair on Finn's back deck, sliding her empty plate away and lifted her water glass to take a sip. "Dinner was delicious, thank you."

"My pleasure. If you want dessert, I'm afraid the best I can do is probably store-bought cookies. I think I still have a box in the cupboard somewhere."

She slanted a look his way. "And here I thought you had something else in mind for dessert."

"Oh, we'll get to that, but we need to chat first. Clear some details up."

Cory opened her eyes fully and stared. "Oh?"

"Don't look so surprised. I said we needed to talk."

"Yeah, but I had begun to think that was a euphemism for sex, or something, since you hadn't said anything earlier, or all through dinner."

Finn smirked. "I was pleasantly distracted, and then I figured it best to have a nice meal first and chat on a full stomach."

Cory tapped her toes against the wooden deck. She rested her arms loosely on the cool metal arms of the chair and returned his gaze. Her mind raced, but she couldn't decipher what he wanted to talk about. "So, spill it, what do you want to discuss?"

Finn rubbed his palms on his jeans and glanced out into the yard at Bat rolling in the grass and then back to Cory.

"It occurred to me, we might be at a point in our relationship where it'd be a good idea to establish some guidelines."

Relationship? He wanted to talk about their relationship. She wrapped her fingers around the arms of the chair. The tapping of her foot increased.

Of course, they had some sort of a relationship. They were neighbors. They had gone out a few times. They'd had sex a couple of times, all right more than a couple if you counted the actual acts rather than the occasion.

She took a breath. "Guidelines? Maybe you should clarify what you mean before my mind jumps to conclusions."

"No big deal, I just think it best to clear the air and make sure we're both on the same page."

Cory sighed. Okay, this she could handle. Typical guy. He was concerned she was getting expectations in her head about them being a couple. Probably worried she would start ordering bridal magazines or something. A tad bit insulting to say the least, but it was normal guy behavior.

"Look, Finn, you have nothing to worry about. There's no need to warn me off or anything."

Finn leaned forward and rested his forearms on his knees. "Warn you off?"

"Yeah, you're obviously worried I'm going to get too attached, and start putting more significance on our relationship than you intended, right?"

"Is that what I meant?" Finn sat back in his chair and folded his arms across his chest. "And there's no worry about that with you because you're what? Scratching an itch? Enjoying your newfound single status?"

Cory blinked and bit her lip. Umm, okay, she was starting to think she had misread the situation. "Exactly what is that supposed to mean?"

"It means exactly what I said. I'm not sure I want to be one of the crowd. A stopover on your road to husband number two."

She lunged to a stand. "One of a crowd? Husband number two? What the hell are you talking about?"

Finn slowly stood and placed his palms on the table. "Don't play games, princess, it's beneath you. I'm talking about Sebastian Marks. What? He's not doing it for you, so you decide to slum a bit?"

Cory narrowed her eyes and folded her arms in front of her waist. "You're lucky I don't smack your face for that. Not sure whom you're insulting more with that accusation, me or you. I'm not dating Sebastian. I had one date with him when I first arrived, that's it. Not sure where you get off accusing me of being a slut and a gold digger. You can go straight to hell, Finn."

She swiveled and stalked down the stairs of the deck and started across the cool grass.

"Damn it! Wait a minute!"

The hard thump of his footsteps pounded across the deck and stairs. The urge to run flashed in her mind before she stopped and swung around. She'd be damned before she ran from anyone.

"What the hell for? You have more insults to hurl my way?"

He stopped in front of her, gazing down at her with his hands on his hips. "I saw him drop you off earlier. Care to explain that?"

"No, I don't. I don't owe you any explanations. Goodbye, Finn." She turned and started back across the lawn.

He grabbed her arm. "Wait."

Cory glared down at his hand on her arm and then back to his face. "Let go."

Finn dropped his hand. "Damn it, Cory. I may be going about this all wrong, but could we please just talk about this rationally?"

"Talk about what? The fact you think I'm a slut or a gold digger?"

Finn ran his hands through his hair roughly. "That's not what I meant. I'm sorry, okay?"

She folded her arms and stared silently.

Finn paced back and forth in front of her. "When I saw you get out of his car...I didn't like it, okay?" He stopped and stared at her. "I don't want you seeing him, or anyone else." He shrugged and opened his arms. "There you have it. I wanted to talk about exclusivity between the two of us."

Cory gripped the sides of her waist and stared off into the woods. "You were jealous."

"Yeah, you want to label it? Fine, I was jealous."

She glanced back at him and away. Scrambling to organize her thoughts, she curled her toes against the cushion of grass beneath her feet. Finn was the casual, good time guy, it never occurred to her he might be interested in a real relationship with her. What chance did that have? Her life was a mess right now. She didn't even know if she would be alive in a few weeks. Her plate was more than full, it was cracking under the strain.

"Say something."

"I'm not sure what to say, Finn."

"Say you're willing to give it a go."

Cory met his gaze. "I don't know if I can right now. I've got a lot going on in my life."

"Does it have anything to do with him?"

"Not in the way you think."

"Then what? What were you doing with him? I should've confronted the bastard like I wanted to this afternoon."

"No!" Cory held up her palm. "Stay away from him." She had no doubt Sebastian could and would kill Finn if he got in the way. "You know what? This isn't going to work. I'm sorry." Cory started backing away and then swung around to jog across the backyard.

He caught up with her at the back door. "Cory, wait, stop."

"No, I'm sorry, but this is over. It's best if you and I go back to being reluctant neighbors." She started moving the pot of flowers by the back door, looking for the key her aunt had once mentioned keeping there. She needed to get inside now, before she lost the tenuous control she had over her emotions.

"Are you afraid of him? Has he hurt you?"

Cory froze and turned around. Finn stood with one foot on the bottom stair and one foot on the ground.

"Answer me, Cory."

She should've let him believe she was involved with Sebastian, but the revulsion was too strong. She had to convince him it was over though.

"No, just stay away from him and me. Please, it's for the best. You need to go." She continued searching the pots, frantic to find the key, before she gave in to the threatening tears.

The creak of the steps and give of the wood planks of the porch announced his ascent rather than retreat. "What the hell are you doing? Cory, I'm not going anywhere until we talk this through. Look at me."

"I'm looking for the damn key!"

He sighed. "It's not there. I convinced her it wasn't safe. I'll tell you where it is after we finish talking."

Cory closed her eyes and tried counting. It didn't work.

She whirled around and gave him her best glare.

He now stood at the top of the stairs watching her.

"Give me the key. There's nothing more to say."

"Oh, I think there's plenty more to say."

"No, there is not." She raised her chin. "You were right, I am seeing Sebastian."

His jaw flexed. "Yeah, the question is why?"

"For the obvious reasons. I told you. You were right."

Finn rubbed his jaw with one hand. "Yeah, see, princess, I don't believe you."

Cory blinked.

"You were pissed when I brought it up before, and then I saw the fear on your face when I mentioned confronting him, and now here you are trying to convince me you're dating him. I'm not buying it. If you won't give me an explanation, then I guess I'll have to go find Marks after all." He turned to go. "Looking forward to it, in fact."

"No!" Cory lunged forward and grabbed his shoulder.

He slowly turned back around, pinning her with his gaze. "Start talking, Cory."

Cory threw her hands up in the air and stared around wildly. She didn't know what to do.

She dropped her face into her hands and fought the desire to start bawling or laughing hysterically. She wasn't sure which urge would win.

She sensed him step toward her, and she moved away, walking down the length of the porch. But she then stopped and faced him.

"You wouldn't believe me if I told you."

"Try me."

"Promise you'll stay far away from Sebastian. Safer if you stay away from me too."

"So far everything you're saying is making me want to find the bastard and pummel him into the ground. You're obviously afraid of him, Cory. What has he done?"

"You must promise to stay away from him. You don't know what he's capable of."

"Then tell me."

"Probably better if I show you." Cory waved her arm toward the holly bushes edging the porch. Branches coated in dark green leaves stretched and lengthened rapidly, shooting across the railing toward Finn.

He jumped back, flinging a hand out against the house to steady himself. He stared at the branches in horror before turning his gaze to Cory.

She waved her arm again, and the branches receded.

"He's a witch, and so am I."

Chapter Twenty-Four

"Okay."

Bile rose in the back of her throat. What had she done? Finn stared at the deck, silent and unmoving. At best, he was probably figuring out the best way to drag her off to the looney bin. At worst, well, at worst he believed her and would want to confront Sebastian. He'd get himself killed.

"Okay, what?"

"When I was twelve, my dad had died a few weeks before, and I had too many emotions I didn't know how to deal with. I fell in with this group of kids that...well to put it mildly they were a bunch of trouble-makers. One day, we'd ditched school and were causing as much mischief as we could get into, graffiti, some vandalism. You get the idea. Anyway, there was this dog in the neighborhood everyone knew to steer clear of. A really nasty bit of work, and so was its owner. We were walking down the sidewalk past the yard that was surrounded by chain-link fence. The dog stood in the middle of the grass watching us. One of the guys yanked my hat off my head and tossed it into the yard with the dog."

His gaze slowly rose to meet hers. "My dad had given me that hat."

Tears pooled in her eyes.

"So, I climbed over the fence. I remember the silence, like everyone and everything was holding its breath. The harsh pounding of my heart echoed in my ears as I inched my way toward my hat, while keeping my gaze firmly fixed on the dog. It didn't move, just watched me. I reached my hat, and slowly bent to grab it. That's when it lunged for me."

Gasping, she clasped a hand over her mouth.

"I turned to run with my hat clutched to my chest, but it snagged the back of my ankle, and I crashed to the ground. I yelled out in pain, and out of the corner of my eye saw the guys scatter. They weren't sticking around for the aftermath. They must have thought for sure I was a goner."

"I heard a low murmuring, and the dog released my ankle. I flipped over and started scrambling backward. The pain shooting up my leg made me cry out. A young woman stood inside the yard. I'd never seen her before. She was staring at the dog and whispering something—no idea what. It wasn't a language I had ever heard. The dog was whining, staring at her. It slowly lowered to its haunches and dropped its head down on its paws. The damnedest thing it was, the dog just fell asleep. I was frozen. The woman ran over to me yanked up the torn leg of my jeans to examine my ankle. She wrapped some cloth around it and asked me if I lived nearby."

He rubbed the back of his neck. "When I nodded, she helped me to stand and asked if I could walk. I wasn't sure, but I wasn't going to say no. The dog started whimpering, and she told me to go. I did. She held out her hand toward the dog and started whispering in that language again. I didn't stop until I was on the other side of the fence. I looked back, and the dog was quiet again. She was gone. Nowhere to be seen. I hobbled home and cleaned up my leg. I never told a soul that story."

A chill danced over Cory's arms, and she rubbed it away.

Finn walked toward her and stopped. "So, what I'm saying is I believe you. I think there's plenty of unexplained things in this world. I'm not saying I understand it, or what it means, but I'd like to try."

She closed her eyes. Tears slid down her cheeks. "My life is a mess."

Warmth encompassed her, as he wrapped his arms around her. She dropped her head onto his chest.

"Tell me."

She told him everything—from discovering her powers to finding out about Sebastian and his father's dark plans.

His arms rubbed her back through the entire explanation, tightening briefly at the mention of Sebastian and his father.

"Anything else?"

She wiped her cheeks and snorted softly. "Isn't that enough?"

"I mean is that everything? You're not holding anything back?"

She showed him the tree symbol on the back of her neck that he had thought was a tattoo. He placed a swift kiss upon it. "Nothing more?"

"No, that's everything."

"You said Melanie was helping you? She find anything out about his family?"

Cory shook her head. "No, not yet. I'm worried she'll draw attention to herself and get hurt. And now I have to worry about you too. Please, promise you'll stay away from this. Stay away from Sebastian."

Finn stared down at her. "You've got to be kidding me. There's no way in hell I'm ever leaving you alone with that guy again. I don't trust him a bit. I'm going with you to these so-called training sessions."

Cory's mouth dropped open and then snapped closed. "Absolutely not! Didn't you hear what I said? He can knock you out with a thought. Most likely kill you with one too." She wrenched herself out of his arms and started pacing across the porch. "I should never have told you about this."

Finn grabbed a hold of her arms and drew her close. "Stop. Yes, you should have, and I'm glad you did. I wasn't about to drop it or let it go. I wasn't letting you go. I don't know what this is between us, but I'm not ready to walk away. We'll deal with all this witch stuff together. You, me, and Melanie, three heads are better than one, right?"

Cory rested her cheek against his shoulder. She didn't know whether to be relieved, or terrified.

"First things first though, I'm going to get the key for Addy's house. I'll be right back, and then you and I will discuss this some more and come up with a plan, okay?"

He waited for her agreement before jogging over to his house. She took a deep breath and straightened her shoulders. He was right, she needed a better plan. She couldn't take back her words or actions, he already knew, so she needed to concentrate on the coming weeks and move forward.

Finn was back in a moment and unlocking the back door. He held the door open for her and she walked past him into the kitchen.

"How about I get us something to drink and we sit down and hash this out?"

"All right but let me run upstairs and check my phone. I should see if Mel or Aunt Addy called while I was over at your house. My aunt should be home any minute, and she knows nothing about this. I insist on keeping it that way."

"Agreed. Grab your shoes and we can head back to my house."

Cory jogged up the stairs and checked her phone. Melanie had called. She played the short voicemail, "Call me as soon as you get this."

Pressing call back, she started to walk back downstairs, but the head-lights of her aunt's car beamed as she entered the driveway. Cory stepped back into her room and closed the door as Mel answered.

"Hey Mel."

"What's wrong?"

Cory sighed. "You know me too well. First tell me why you wanted me to call."

"Okay, but only because I've been dying to tell you. You will tell me after, right?"

"Yeah."

"I found Sebastian's family. His father's name is Edward Marks. Here's the sketchy thing, no birth certificate, no social security number, no trace of his identity anywhere. I found him by tracing Sebastian. There was an obscure mention of Sebastian attending a charity fundraiser along with other members of the Marks family including his father and sister. His sister's name is Miranda. He has a brother too, Miles. I discovered a foundation the Marks family runs, but every time I try to uncover more information, I hit more walls. Not surprisingly, they're very secretive. I found proof of an Edward Marks in England during the seventeenth century. I'm not one hundred percent positive it's the same one, but I'm waiting for more reference material which should tell me either way. It corroborates Sebastian's story if it is indeed him."

"I wonder if the sister is the one Sebastian is protecting."

"Yeah, if he was telling the truth, and not giving you a line of bull-shit to make him sound more human and capable of caring for anyone beyond himself."

"Good point."

"So what has you sounding so glum?"

The soft murmur of Finn's and her aunt's voices in the kitchen drifted up the stairs. She rested her forehead against the closed bedroom door. "I told Finn everything."

Silence stretched across the phone. "Good."

"Good? How can that be good, Mel?"

"Because you're not alone up there. I've been trying to decide where I do the most good helping you. I've been torn between rushing up there to be by your side and trying to do all the research from there or staying put here and having greater access to information. Knowing Finn will be there to help you...wait, he will be there to help you, right? The bastard didn't turn tail and run, did he?"

A miniscule chuckle escaped her. "No, Mel, he didn't run. He's insisting on accompanying me for my sessions with Sebastian. He doesn't want me alone with him."

"Hallelujah! Good for him and you."

"Is it really? And what if he gets hurt, or killed?"

"Stop taking the world on your shoulders, Cory. You probably couldn't stop him from going, anyway. People make their own choices and decisions. The important question is do you trust him with your secret and to be there for you?"

"Yes." There was no hesitation. She trusted him with her secrets and her life.

"Then let him have your back. Now, what can I do to help you?"

"Keep digging, carefully, into the Marks family. The more knowledge I have, the better. I'm going to step up the training schedule with Sebastian, and on my own. I'm not relying on him to teach me everything I need to know."

"Excellent."

"Be safe, Mel."

"You too, Cory."

Cory disconnected the call. She slipped her phone into her pocket and opened the door. Straightening her spine, she headed down the stairs.

She had a name to focus her rage on. If Edward Marks came for her, he would be in for a battle.

A surge of energy erupted through her veins. She grasped the railing as it spread to her fingertips and toes.

The power was there, waiting. She would learn to harness and use it. God help anyone who harmed those she loved.

Chapter Twenty-Five

"What's one more dead body to dispose of?" Sebastian shrugged and placed his hands in the pockets of his pants.

Cory squeezed Finn's hand, hoping he wouldn't lose his temper and try to strike out at Sebastian.

"Listen, you arrogant prick, I don't trust you. I'll be damned if Cory's life will be in your hands. You can make all the threats you want. I could make some too, but that won't protect Cory or teach her what she needs to learn. So, how about we skip the posturing bullshit and get to her training and the plan to thwart your evil family's intentions?"

"On that note..." Cory released Finn's hand and rubbed his shoulder. "You promised to observe only, and it's best if you do it from a distance. Please go wait in your car and remember your promise not to interfere. "

Finn stared down at Cory for a moment, before pressing a kiss to her forehead. A brief glare at Sebastian, then he spun away and stalked to his car. Instead of getting in, he folded his arms and leaned against the door.

Cory sighed, glanced at the ground a moment, straightened her shoulders, and faced Sebastian. "Let's get started."

"Excellent suggestion," an unknown voice echoed across the meadow.

Cory whirled to her right to face the intruder. Scratch that, intruders. A man and two women stepped from the woods into the meadow.

Sebastian sauntered toward them, stopping several feet away. His hands still remained in his pants' pockets.

Was he not concerned? Did he know them? Had he betrayed her?

Finn appeared at her side.

"Hello Miles, Miranda, Willow. What, may I ask, are you doing here?"

The man stepped forward and spread his hands out. "Cleaning up your mess little brother. Father has lost confidence in you."

Cory gripped Finn's hand. They needed to run.

Before they could, a strong gust of wind swept them both up and slammed them to the ground.

"You're not going anywhere, Miss Bishop."

She lifted her head. Finn surged to his feet. Before he could take a step, Sebastian waved a hand, and Finn dropped to the ground. She stared in terror, the breath frozen in her chest until she saw the slight rise and fall of his own.

Alive but unconscious.

Panted breaths sawed from her chest. Her fingernails filled with dirt as she clenched her fingers in the ground preparing to rise.

Sebastian had betrayed their bargain. "Bargain?"

The woman in the center tilted her head to the side. Her long brown hair cascaded over the side of her face as she stared toward Cory.

"What is it, Miranda?" Miles' gaze was pinned on Cory.

Miranda's mouth and eyes widened in horror before she dropped to the ground unconscious.

Miles glanced down at her and then swung his gaze back up to Sebastian. Sebastian threw out his arms, and Miles flew backward like he was yanked by a bungee cord. He smashed into a tree and crumpled to the ground.

Sebastian ran to the woman left standing, watching the scene unfold with a detached air. "Willow, you need to run—now. Take my car."

Suddenly her body soared through the air, landing in a heap on the ground. She moaned in pain but made no move to get up.

Sebastian spun back to Miles.

"I must say, you've surprised me little brother. Betraying our father? Your family? Starting a battle, you cannot win? You've drained your power knocking out so many at once, brother. How can you possibly hope to best me on your own? Little Willow is useless in a fight."

Vines slithered across the ground and dropped from branches wrapping around Miles' wrists and ankles. His body was wrenched up like a rag doll, and his arms and legs were yanked apart as he was suspended in midair.

"He's not alone." Cory slowly stood.

Sebastian glanced over his shoulder at her. "Be ready. That won't hold him long. Miles' power comes from the air. He can control the weather." He gestured at Miranda, still on the ground unconscious. "Miranda is a telepath, also of the air, she read your mind. If she comes to, you must block your thoughts, or she'll know your next move. Leave Willow be, understood?"

Electricity coursed through the surrounding air. Wind whipped against Cory. She glanced up at Miles straining against the vines. His eyes were closed, his head tilted back, his mouth moved, but she couldn't hear the words over the rising wind.

Vines snapped.

Cory sent a surge of power to the vines trying to hold them together.

Lightning flashed above them. Thunder rumbled.

The wind shoved her back a step, and then another, before she caught her balance and planted her feet. She looked up to see Miles standing free about fifty feet away from her. Sebastian stood ten feet to her right. He looked up at the sky and smiled.

"A mistake to bring a storm, Miles."

A deluge of rain fell from the sky, all centered on Miles.

Lightning struck the ground in rapid succession, closer and closer to where they stood.

Sebastian threw out his hands. The rain changed to ice, pelting Miles like thousands of shards of glass. He fell to his knees and opened his arms wide staring up at the sky.

Cory sent every ounce of power she could muster to roots and vines to contain him.

Thunder crashed above.

The hairs on her arms stood on end. A blur of yellow sped by.

Finn's Mustang rammed into Miles and sent him flying through the air.

The thunder stopped. The wind died. An eerie calm blanketed the area.

Cory collapsed to the ground.

Finn exited his car and ran to her, dropping to his knees in front of her and wrapping his arms around her body. She sank against him, spent.

Sebastian was on all fours next to them, gasping from exertion. He glanced over at them. "Nice timing, D'Orsey."

Finn lunged at Sebastian, punching him in the jaw. "If you hadn't knocked me out, I could've helped a lot sooner."

Sebastian rolled over and sprawled on the ground face up. "If I hadn't knocked you out, barely mind you, then you would be dead. Miles would've killed you first to send Coralea into an emotional tailspin. You should thank me for saving your life, but considering your timely action let's say we're even."

Cory flung her arm out and grabbed Finn's arm. He looked at her and gathered her back into his arms. "Are you all right?"

"Yes, just exhausted. A little bruised, but nothing serious."

Sebastian slowly staggered to his feet.

"What are you doing?"

"Making sure the bastard is dead."

"He's not," a soft voice whispered. Willow hesitantly approached them.

Finn helped Cory to her feet. Sebastian looked at Willow and then to the woods where Miles should have been. They all followed the direction of his gaze.

Miles was gone and so was Miranda.

The three of them searched in every direction and braced for an attack.

"You're safe—for now. They left."

Sebastian stumbled slightly as he walked over to the woman. She gave him a small smile, and he hugged her closely. They both turned and faced Finn and Cory.

"Willow, this is Coralea Bishop and Finnegan D'Orsey. This is my sister, Willow. She's my twin."

Willow whispered a shy, "Hello."

Finn gave a short nod in greeting, and Cory attempted a small smile. Delicate was the first word that came to mind gazing at Willow. She was slender with pale blonde hair, and light skin.

Sebastian glanced down at the top of Willow's head tucked against him. "What have you seen?"

Cory wrapped her arms around Finn's waist and collapsed against him. Her limbs dragged like anchors. Her energy depleted, she wanted to crawl into his arms and forget all about today, but first she needed answers. "How do you know we are safe for now? What if they circle back, or get reinforcements?"

Sebastian raised his hand. "Hold off for a moment. Willow's power is premonition. If she says we're safe for now, then we are."

"Okay, but you really need to explain everything to me, not just these bits and pieces you've been doling out."

Sebastian sighed. "A full coven comprises twelve because there are twelve central powers, three for each of the four elements. Air is manipulation over the weather, telepathy, or telekinesis. Fire is the manipulation of fire, healing, or mind control. Water is the manipulation of water, premonition, or the ability to communicate with aquatic life. Earth is plant manipulation, ability to communicate with animals, or the ability to manipulate the earth."

Cory focused on Willow. "You can see the future?"

Willow frowned. "I get random images. I don't often know what they mean, or how to put them together and interpret them. I don't have any control over what I see." She shrugged. "Pretty useless."

Sebastian grasped her shoulders and directed her to face him. "That's not true. You told us we're safe for now. That gives us time to recharge and come up with a plan. Tell me what you saw."

"I saw the confrontation today, that's how I knew your plan to oppose father. I knew you would win today, so I wasn't afraid when father ordered Miles to come collect you and the heir. I've also seen

Miles and Miranda back with father. Miles is hurt badly, but I think he recovers."

"Any sort of timeline with these premonitions?" Finn asked. "Because if this reprieve is giving us time to heal and plan, it's doing the same for them."

Willow shook her head. "No. I'm sorry."

"Don't be sorry, you've helped. We still have some time before the eclipse. Father will regroup and come for Coralea again. He has to, he needs her power to strengthen his. We need to be ready."

"No."

They all looked at Willow.

Willow peeked up at Sebastian as a tear slipped down her cheek.

"What is it, Willow?"

"I gave him someone else."

Chapter Twenty-Six

Willow crumpled against Sebastian, her soft sobs drenching his shirt. Sebastian held his sister tight and closed his eyes. It was the most real emotion Cory had ever witnessed from him.

She and Finn shared a glance. He rubbed her upper arm, and she gave him a gentle hug. "What does she mean, Sebastian?"

Sebastian murmured something to Willow and then met Cory and Finn's gaze. "Part of Willow's abilities involve visions of others with power. Father exploits her abilities in order to locate witches he can use."

Willow raised her tear-streaked face. "One of the few reasons he keeps me around. My only other use to him is to help control Sebastian. If I didn't exist, he could have disappeared a long time ago. I'm the noose around his neck."

"Hush, little one, that's not true. You've kept me relatively sane all these years. Besides, disappearing isn't realistic, at least not for long, anyway. Father would find us."

"This ability is how you found me?"

Willow met Cory's gaze with a sideways glance before she looked at the ground and nodded.

Sebastian tightened his arm around Willow's shoulders. "It's not as cut and dried as it seems. Willow only knew Josephine's heir was here.

She didn't know who it was, or if you had discovered your power. I was sent to find you. I was the one who traced the line to Adelaide and got close to her. I made sure I was there the day you arrived. I sensed the power buried inside you."

"So, you what, decided to date me? To what end? When did you decide to train me to go against your father?"

"I'd already had a plan in my head before we met, but I had no idea whether you were strong enough. I needed a way to get close to you, and dating was the easiest, and most enjoyable option. Of course, D'Orsey here kept getting in the way."

Finn took a step closer to Sebastian, but Cory quickly stepped between them. "You're a real piece of work, Marks," Finn snarled.

Cory shook her head. "It doesn't matter at this point. What I want to know is what happens now, and what about this other person Willow gave him?"

Sebastian sighed. "Well that depends on whether Father finds this person, and whether they have enough power to satisfy him. Now that Miles and Miranda know you exist and have power, you can bet they'll be rushing home to tell Father."

"He wants Justin." Willow wiped the tears from her cheeks and wrapped her arms around herself.

Sebastian looked down at his sister. "Who's Justin?"

"The one in my vision, Justin Crown. He is of the Earth as well, but he can manipulate it. He's demonstrated his power. I told Father about him because I had a vision you would go against him, and Coralea would help you. I knew Father would switch his efforts to Justin once I told him about the earthquake he had caused since he didn't know who you were or if you had power."

Cory gasped. "Earthquake? He caused an earthquake?"

Willow cringed and nodded.

"Father would definitely want him." Sebastian rubbed his chin and sighed.

"Yes, he left as soon as I told him. He told Miles to come check on you, and then join him. Miles only took me along because there was no one left at home to watch me."

Finn wrapped an arm around Cory's shoulders. "Does this mean Cory is safe?"

Cory glanced up at Finn and then back to Sebastian and Willow.

"Only for the short term. She'll never be safe as long as our father is alive. She'll always be a target."

Finn spun away and pounded his fist on the roof of his car. Cory winced.

What were her options? Running? Sebastian made it clear there was nowhere to run Edward Marks wouldn't find her. She had to learn to protect herself and those she loved. She needed to destroy Edward Marks.

Willow stepped forward. "We're all targets. We need to help one another in order to survive. We need to find others to join us in this fight. It's the only way."

They all stared at Willow.

Sebastian sighed. "Have you seen this?"

"No, I don't need a vision to know this. We can't run, Sebastian. We need to stop him. We can't let him ruin any other lives."

Cory stepped forward and touched Willow's slender shoulder. "I agree."

"Great, you agree. Do either of you have any sort of plan? How are we going to stop him? Better question is how are we going to stay alive?" Sebastian headed for his car. "I need some damn water."

"I didn't tell Father Justin's last name. I told him where he was when he created the earthquake, but that's not where he is now. We have some time, not much, but some."

Sebastian paused and looked back at her. "You're amazing, Willow. You did buy us time. Miles' injuries buy us some more time, but we need to stay focused." He continued to his car and drank a couple of bottles of water. He returned and handed each of them a bottle.

After taking a large swallow, Finn leaned back against his car. "It seems to me the first order of business is building our defenses so we're ready when and if they do come."

Sebastian glared.

Cory nodded at Finn. "Willow is right. We need to find others. We need to build our own coven."

Chapter Twenty-Seven

Finn's warm hand rested on her naked hip. Cory's fingers idly caressed his bare chest as she rested her head against his shoulder. They'd parted ways with Sebastian and Willow and arrived back at Finn's where they shared a shower and ended up in bed making love.

"You're very quiet, well except for the little scream earlier after you demanded I give it to you harder."

Cory lightly slapped him on the chest. Finn chuckled and held her closer.

"I can't stop thinking about it. Someone else is taking my place. Some innocent man is going to lose his life instead of me. I can't live with that, Finn."

"First of all, you don't know if he's an innocent or not. Secondly, none of it is your choice or fault. Third, it hasn't happened yet."

"I have to help him."

Finn sighed. "Yeah, I kind of figured you were going to say that, and it's we. We will help him. I already reached out to a buddy I have before I joined you in the shower. He's going to track down this guy and get us all the information he can on him."

Cory stretched to plant a kiss on his lips. "Thank you. What about Sebastian and Willow?"

"What about them?"

"Willow was pretty broken up about serving this Justin Crown guy up to her father. She told Sebastian they had to find him first, before their father."

"Yeah, well, I don't think Sebastian was too keen on the idea. He's more concerned about keeping Willow and himself safe from the rest of their family."

"Well, they've basically declared war against the rest of their crazy family. Who knows what the repercussions from that will be."

"Exactly why we need to take precautions. Who knows what they will try next. I don't think we've seen the last of them."

Cory rested her chin on his chest and peeked up at him. "You keep saying we, are you sure you want to be a part of my insane life? I wouldn't blame you a bit if you kept your distance from me."

Finn rolled his eyes. "Not this again. Listen up, princess, I'm in this for the long haul. Got it? I'd be lying if I said this magic shit didn't throw me for a bit of a loop, but it doesn't change the way I feel about you."

"Oh? And how do you feel about me?"

Finn smirked at her. "You want the words, huh? I thought actions spoke louder than words."

Stacking her hands underneath her chin she smiled. "I want the words. Your actions show me you're brave and a bit crazy. You could just have a thing for a damsel in distress."

A soft snort and a bark of laughter escaped him. "You? A damsel in distress? The same woman who caged and suspend a powerful witch who controlled the weather? I don't see you as a damsel in distress, princess."

"Good, just keep that image in mind if you ever cheat on me. I'll make that look like child's play."

Finn rolled her over and rose above her grinning. "See, that's the proper response if you're significant other betrays you."

Cory rolled her eyes. "I threaten you with bodily harm, and it makes you happy?"

"Mm-hmm, and horny, don't forget horny." Finn captured her lips for a scorching kiss.

She looped her arms around his neck. "Still waiting on the words."

He stared down into her eyes. "I love you. I love everything about you. Your strength, honor, loyalty, heart, and passion. The fire that burns inside you and lights up the room every time you walk in. Your smokin' hot body doesn't hurt either."

Finn laughed as Cory swatted at him through the tears in her eyes. "I love you too, for your bravery, honor, and strength." She ran her hands down his sides. "And your smokin' hot body too."

He placed a soft kiss on her lips. Cory licked her lips. "It's not over."

"No, but we'll take it one day at a time and we will stand together. " Cory whispered, "together."

THANK you for reading Legacy of Magic! If you enjoyed the story, please consider leaving a review.

LEGACY OF DESTRUCTION continues the Legacy series with Willow and Justin.

SIGN up for my newsletter to be the first to hear about new releases, sales, giveaways, and other exclusive content! http://eepurl.com/dt5N7M

About the Author

Denise Carbo writes Romance and Women's Fiction. She is a voracious reader, loves to travel, and is fascinated by the supernatural.

She lives in a small, picturesque, New England town with her high school sweetheart and their three amazing sons. Find out more at https://www.DeniseCarbo.com and sign up for her newsletter to be the first to hear about new books, sales, giveaways, and exclusive content. https://eepurl.com/dt5N7M

Also by Denise Carbo

www.ingramcontent.com/pod-product-compliance
Lightning Source LLC
Chambersburg PA
CBHW020333260626
47156CB00004B/1507